"I should have known that a guy like you wouldn't be my date. I don't know where my head was." Scarlett looked at Luke and shook her head.

Now, what was that supposed to mean?

She stood up before he could ask. "Listen, I am really sorry about messing things up here. Take me back to the island and I'll get out of your hair. You can track down your real contact and get back to your mission."

"Uh...Scarlett, I really don't know how to tell you this but, see, you went through security with me. You might not be my contact, but you *are* my fiancée. At least for the next three days. I absolutely cannot let you walk out of here."

Books by Susan May Warren

Love Inspired Suspense   Steeple Hill

SUSAN MAY WARREN

is a RITA® Award-winning, bestselling novelist of more than twenty-five novels. She has won an Inspirational Readers Choice Award, an ACFW Book of the Year award and has been a Christy Award finalist. Her compelling plots and unforgettable characters have won her acclaim with readers and reviewers alike. She and her husband of twenty years and their four children live in a small town on Minnesota's beautiful Lake Superior shore, where they are active in their local church. You can find her online at www.susanmaywarren.com.

UNDERCOVER PURSUIT

SUSAN MAY WARREN

Love Inspired

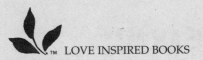 LOVE INSPIRED BOOKS

Recycling programs for this product may not exist in your area.

ISBN-13: 978-0-373-44440-3

UNDERCOVER PURSUIT

www.LoveInspiredBooks.com

Printed in U.S.A.

Forgetting the past and looking forward to
what lies ahead, I press on to reach the end of the race
and receive the heavenly prize for which God
through Jesus Christ is calling us.
                              —*Philippians* 3:13, 14

For Your glory, Lord

ONE

How could she have lost her sister's wedding dress?

Scarlett Hanson closed her eyes, willing herself not to leap across the customer service counter of AirMexico airlines and throttle the petite brunette airline representative in her cute light blue uniform and pigtails, typing a description of Scarlett's lost "suitcase" into her computer.

"It's not in a suitcase," Scarlett repeated. "It's a black, zippered hanging bag, with a pink ribbon on the handle, and please, please, my sister will kill me if you can't find it." Scarlett spread her sweaty hands on the cool smooth counter, aware of the line forming behind her. The rest of the passengers on Flight 2137 had already cleared customs, the officers at the customs desks now resuming conversations with their colleagues while the next bunch of tourists from the icy north herded through passport control. Beyond the glass doors, she spotted palm trees and cabbies in Hawaiian shirts, shorts and flip-flops, peddling freedom.

"Contents?"

"It's a wedding dress!" Oh, she hadn't meant to yell, but that's what sixteen hours of travel on nothing more than a bag of peanuts and a Diet Coke did. It didn't help that she'd had about six hours' notice before that to block out vacation time at her temp agency, pack, pick up her sister's dress—as well as her maid-of-honor dress—from a Nicollet Mall boutique in Minneapolis and catch her flight.

She just needed to calm down. Everything was going to be *just fine*. Hadn't her flight made it out before the storms across the nation had grounded other flights? If that wasn't divine providence—allowing her to make it onto the overbooked connection in Houston—then she didn't know what was.

See, just because she felt as if God had forgotten her didn't mean it was true. He did care about her, and she didn't have to be a high-maintenance, high-stress, center-of-the-world diva like Bridgett to prove it.

Although, having her sister's dress suddenly appear might prove God's attention to the details.

"Are you sure the bag isn't listed on the manifest?" She wanted to bang her head on the counter. Why hadn't she carried her sister's dress on the plane instead of checking it?

Or better, why hadn't Scarlett just let her sister's frantic phone call go to voice mail two days ago?

Maybe because, after the fiasco at the engagement party, she just wanted to make things right.

Scarlett's feet had begun to sweat in her Uggs. She should have left her ski jacket in the parking garage at the Minneapolis/St. Paul airport. Please let her have remembered her swimsuit—although knowing Bridgett, the bride wouldn't have scheduled beach time. Just lots of it's-all-about-Bridgett time.

Scarlett shed the jacket and shoved it into the expandable pocket of her carry-on bag.

"Oh, I found it!" Pigtails peered at the screen, squinting. "It's— oh, no…"

Scarlett gripped the counter, leaning forward, hoping for a glimpse of the screen. "What's 'oh, no'?"

"It's in…Detroit."

Detroit. Of course it was.

Maybe it wasn't too late to catch a return flight back to the States.

"We can have it here by tomorrow, probably, Saturday at the latest."

"She's getting married Saturday morning."

Pigtails smiled, white teeth against her beautifully tanned skin. "If you leave the name of your hotel, we can send it out to you when it arrives."

Perfect. Scarlett dug out her cell phone and scrolled down to the notes. "The Lost Breezes Hotel."

"You know that isn't actually in Cancun, right? You have to take a ferry out to the island." The woman glanced behind her at the clock. "Oh, you'd better hurry. The last ferry to the island leaves in thirty minutes."

Of course it did. Scarlett grabbed one of the business cards on the counter. "I'll call you when I get to the resort."

"We hope you enjoy your stay in Cancun," Pigtails said, her eyes already tracking to the complainer behind her.

At this point, Scarlett had her doubts.

She practiced some deep breathing, not glancing at the clock as she lined up to go through customs.

The agent seemed to pity her—or perhaps he just recognized a woman fraying as he released her and her carry-on bag into the country.

Welcome to Mexico. She passed the sign and entered a corridor, bordered by all manner of tourist services—

tropical-colored signs advertising tours of lost coves and white-sand beaches, luxury golf packages, deep-sea fishing charters. She trolleyed her bag, the one with the chipped wheel that made a clipping sound as she walked, ignoring the calls of eager agents hoping to sell her a chance to swim with dolphins, learn to scuba dive or cook Mexican cuisine.

Thanks, but she was here for one reason: erase that horrid moment at the engagement party when she'd accused Bridgett of stealing Duncan, the groom.

Stealing—had she really used that word? That was the last time she drank champagne. Ever. One glass and her mouth stopped listening to her brain.

Scarlett smiled at a group of taxi drivers lingering in the cool air-conditioning of the airport and exited out onto the sidewalk. Her sister said a marked taxi would be waiting to take her and the last of the groomsmen to the resort.

Please, don't let Bridgett have set her up on a blind date. Scarlett could see right through Bridgett's pitiful attempts over the past six months to set her up, straight to the guilty conscience behind it. But there was no need for it. She and Duncan had never—not really—been a couple. Officially.

Regardless of the hours they spent hanging out after the church singles group events.

Regardless of the times they played tennis, or went cross-country skiing.

And, especially, regardless of what Scarlett may or may not have said at the engagement party.

No, she would be just fine at this wedding as a solo act. Singular. Dateless.

Sigh.

Scarlett had never seen palm trees. They lined the

circular boulevard outside the airport. But she must have been miles from the ocean because she couldn't smell anything but exhaust.

Lost Breezes—there. She spotted a Hispanic man in a white silk shirt, jeans and flip-flops holding a laminated sign. "Lost Breezes?" she asked in English.

He smiled. *"Si."*

"Gracias." Finally, she might be able to use her four years of high-school Spanish

He reached for her bag. Wait—hadn't she read something about people masquerading as cabbies and running off with carry-ons? She held her bag tighter. "I'll take it in the car with me," she said—or hoped she said—in Spanish.

He raised an eyebrow, then shrugged and opened the door of his sedan.

Indeed, the foreshadowed guest sat inside, waiting— impatiently, if she could read his body language. He looked over at her, his lips pursed, his eyes dark, sweat dampening the front of his white Oxford dress shirt. He wore a pair of jeans and black Converse sneakers, and made a feeble attempt to hide his irritation.

"Hi. Sorry I'm late." She set the carry-on on the floor then climbed in around it.

He gave her a tight smile. "Hi." He eyed her Uggs and possibly her turtleneck, but it was two degrees in Rochester, thank you very much. Just get her to a beach.

She sat back and noticed that, despite his perspiration, he didn't exactly smell bad. And, upon closer inspection, she might even call him cute—tousled dark blond hair, golden-brown eyes, and it seemed he might spend some time in the gym. There was confidence in his posture, despite his impatience, as if he expected the world to be on time. And dressed appropriately. Exactly the kind of guy who might be interested in Bridgett.

Or, the kind of guy who might be her sister's cast-off. Oh, no, please—

"I'm Luke. You must be my date." He offered his hand to her.

She knew it. For goodness' sake. She would kill Bridgett when she saw her.

"Okay. Well, I'm Scarlett. And I don't know what you were told, but I'm just here for the wedding. So, you're off the hook, pal. You don't have to be my plus-one." She gave him a tight smile, ignoring his hand.

He withdrew his hand and gave her a look. "Scarlett. Okay. I admit, I heard you like to work solo, but hey, I'm here to do a job, same as you. So, no, I don't think I'm *off the hook,* thanks."

Wow, that hurt. She liked to work solo? A job? What had her sister said to this guy? She liked a date just as much as the next girl. Just because she hadn't had one in…well, her friendship with Duncan had nixed any real offers. Still, being her date for the weekend was a "job"? "Thanks, but I just want to get this over with as painlessly as possible. So, really, I don't need your help."

And she didn't. With the exception of the dress— which had to make it in on the next plane—she could handle this wedding with her eyes closed. Nothing short of a terrorist attack would keep her from making sure Bridgett had the wedding of her dreams, and paying the appropriate attention to her "date" would only dilute her focus. She put some sugar in her tone, however, because no man—especially one of Bridgett's pals—liked getting shut out. "Thanks for the offer, though. I'll give you a good report, I promise." Then, as the taxi pulled away from the curb into the mess of traffic, she winked at him. No hard feelings.

He stared at her as if she'd slapped him. "Wow. You really think you're something, don't you?"

"Uh…"

"Well, guess what? You're not getting rid of me quite that easily. For the next three days, I'm your partner, whether you like it or not. So buckle up, honey."

Awesome. She'd landed her own personal hero. Just what she needed.

Luke Dekker hated working a mission with an operative he didn't know. He'd read Stacey—er, Scarlett, apparently, was the name she'd chosen for this op— Meyer's dossier on the plane on the way over, and while she seemed capable on paper, meeting her in person had him second-guessing the entire assignment. *Really, I don't need your help.*

And now she looked at him with unadulterated horror on her face, as if he'd just propositioned her.

Luke had been to Cancun before. The first time was a spring-break trip in high school that he barely remembered. Not that he really wanted to remember anything from those days. Still, he didn't recall the small houses amidst towering resort hotels, palm trees and cracked sidewalks, dusty children playing in dirt lots, but maybe no one saw the back alleys of Cancun unless they really looked.

"I really do know what I'm doing. This isn't my first time around the block." He smiled, trying to lighten things up. Somehow, he'd gotten off on the wrong foot with her. Maybe because he kept sticking the other one in his mouth.

She looked even more offended, her eyes blinking.

"Well, I'm sure it's not." Then she closed her mouth and turned away from him, shaking her head as if trying to dislodge his words.

What sort of penance was this? So maybe he shouldn't have mouthed off when his boss, Chet Stryker, asked for volunteers for a mission to Cancun. *"Hey, I need a tan, Chet."* Did the guy not know sarcasm when he heard it?

Only, maybe the joke was on him, because in the six-hour turnaround where he threw something that resembled swim trunks and wrinkled dress clothes from the back of his closet into his bag, he hadn't even considered he might end up working with a snow queen.

Hopefully she packed her sunscreen, because the woman wore the hue—and demeanor—of Minnesota in January.

But he wasn't here to be just an accessory, thanks. This was just as much his mission as hers. And, despite Miss I-Work-Alone's confidence, the woman needed someone to watch her back as she pretended to be a bridesmaid. She'd be busy enough inserting herself into the bridal party of Lucia Romero, bride to Benito Sanchez, nephew of Augusto Sanchez, wanted drug lord and human-trafficking terrorist—and esteemed member of the guest list.

Lucia, a former law student, had been playing loving girlfriend to Benito for three years just for the chance to apprehend Augusto. And now, someone was trying to kill her. She needed people around her who she could trust to keep an eye on things until Augusto showed up to the wedding and the good guys used the opportune rare appearance to swoop in and nab him.

Hence, Lucia had turned to her old friend Chet Stryker and his international-security team. But Stryker

International needed a few more female operatives on its team, because its only official female member had a severe bout of morning sickness.

Although, Mae, Chet's wife, had nearly gotten on the plane with Luke this morning anyway. Even when Chet told her he'd brought in an accomplished freelancer to partner with Luke. A real pro, no problem. Stacey Meyer.

A pro who preferred to work solo, according to her file. Her description, however, hadn't quite done her justice. Sure, the woman beside him didn't exactly qualify as striking, but she had a prettiness about her, something simple and muted that could probably get her in and out of countries unnoticed. She wore her brown hair in a messy ponytail, some of it waterfalling around her face, and her intense green eyes suggested she could turn a person cold with a look. The way she seemed to scrutinize everything, from the driver to the landscape to Luke, as if taking in every detail...yes, he had no doubt she knew how to do her job alone. But too bad. "Listen, I know this isn't your first choice. Frankly, it's not mine, either—"

"What, there were other choices? A lottery?"

"No. I mean, I volunteered. But I was also the only one available."

"Nice. I didn't realize you guys were in such demand."

What had Chet gotten him into? "I stay pretty busy."

She widened her eyes a moment, a flare of something he might normally peg as panic.

"Please, just stay away from me." She looked down at the space between them, then scooted more toward the window and crossed her arms and legs. A knot of offended female pride.

Or…maybe this was about the *job*. She probably feared that he'd take advantage of his role as her fiancé.

Staying away might be a little difficult if they hoped to pull off this charade. Yet, because she was still staring out the window, still shaking her head in a sort of disbelief, he lowered his voice. "Listen, I'm a good guy, really, and I won't take advantage. And I know I'm not who you expected, but I'm not interested in anything but doing my job. We'll just get it done and go home."

She turned, and just for a moment she looked as if she might slap him. "How can I thank you for that ever-so-sweet warning, and for being willing to do this oh-so-offensive job? What would the world do without heroes like you?"

Ow.

But that's what did it. The last thing he needed was a hotshot agent who had to run her own show. "Listen, I'm not just here to watch," he said, slipping into his navy SEAL bark. "I'm here for a reason, same as you, which will probably include not only being near you, but probably even *touching* you." He spent a little extra time on the word *touching,* just because of the price-less expression on her face. He probably shouldn't have smiled, though.

"You'd *better* just be watching. I can give you my deathbed word that there won't be anything but *watching* going on, buddy." She shot a look at his hands as if they'd wandered somewhere. "Touch me once and you'll pull away a nub."

Oh! Uh. No, he hadn't meant—now he felt like a letch.

Which made all the anger dissolve. He wasn't that guy. She actually looked as if he'd offended her, her eyes reddening just a bit. So much for the iceberg agent.

"Look, I'm sorry—"

"Let's just get to the wedding and try to stay out of each other's way."

"Yeah, *that's* going to work."

She took a breath, and it trembled on exhale. "I really, really don't need an escort, you know. No matter what anyone says."

Oh, he wanted to punch something, hard. "I'm not sure you quite cleared that up for me."

"Jerk."

Just swell. They'd have to start acting like a couple soon, because the moment they got on the island, Sanchez's men were sure to be watching. "You could try to cooperate."

"Cooperate. You want me to cooperate. Okay, this is me, cooperating. I'm the queen of cooperating." She drew in a long breath, then bit her lip and, if he wasn't mistaken, she tried not to…cry?

And right then, he had the strangest urge to push that errant dark caramel curl of hair away from her face, turn her toward him. Look right into her eyes.

Look who wasn't as tough as she thought.

Interesting. He wasn't sure what buttons he'd pushed, but something had her rattled.

He and Chet were going to have a long chat when he got to the resort. But he'd come a long way since the navy had discharged him for his temper, and he now had a let's-play-nicely-with-others voice. "We both know what's expected, and I promise, I'm going to watch your back if you watch mine. So let's make the best of it, try to get along. How about we start over?" He put out his hand. "Nice to meet you, Scarlett."

She glanced over at him and sighed. "Fine. Nice to meet you, Luke."

That was a start. "Aren't you hot?"

Her eyes darted to her turtleneck then over to him and his cotton Oxford.

Finally, she said, "Okay, yes, I'm boiling. I should have layered, so I could have shed as I came south, but I was in a hurry. I didn't even get the call that I was coming here until…I guess almost two days ago now, and I had so much to do that, well, I forgot to dress for the weather." She lifted one of her feet, probably marinating inside her blue fuzzy boots.

"Yeah, I only found out yesterday. Good thing we could put this together so fast."

"So, you didn't know you were coming, either? Aren't you in the wedding party?" She regathered her hair into its ponytail, then fanned her face with a business card she held in her hand. For an operative, she had a small-town look about her—a sprinkle of freckles on a small nose, a little extra padding on her—instead of the hard-edged, lean-bodied look of a woman who could flip him in hand-to-hand combat. She looked just normal enough that they might pull this thing off.

"No. I'm just here for you." He winked at her, and again, she gave him the oddest look, one that made him lose his smile.

"I thought you were a groomsman."

"No, that's not part of the plan. But you're a bridesmaid, right?"

She nodded, staring again out the window. "Except my maid-of-honor dress fits someone else. I probably won't eat for three days. If it even gets here." She sighed and leaned back. "I can't take any more glitches." She shook her head.

Glitches?

A mariachi band from the driver's radio filled the silence.

What glitches? "Is it something I should be worried about?"

"I think we'll live through it."

Good. Because survival always topped his priority list.

She closed her eyes, as if she weren't worried, either.

Fine. Okay. He stared out the window as the cabbie drove them through the city.

At least she had stopped calling him names.

The driver let them off at the ferry entrance, and as she wrestled her carry-on out of the car—Luke offered to do it, but she'd rebuffed him—he bought their tickets.

"It's leaving, come on!" He took off, but that crazy bag she'd opted for—which completed the tourist façade well but made him want to throw it in the ocean— clip-clopped over the deck and down the cement pier. He finally returned for it and picked it up.

"I can take it."

"I'm sure you can, but we can't miss the ferry." He gestured to the man waiting for them and didn't put down the bag until they had climbed aboard and gone to the top deck.

"Thank you." She sat on the bench and breathed out, lifting her face to the sun. "I'm sorry for being on edge. I just don't like surprises. And, frankly, you're not what I expected."

"What did you expect?" Hadn't she been given his file to read also?

She gave him a small smile, a shake of her head. "I'm just used to…it's just better if I go it alone."

Yeah, well. "I prefer it, too, actually."

She sighed. "I don't *like* it. It's just the way it is."

He sat next to her, breathing in the salty air and the tang of coconut oil, listening to the cry of gulls overhead. The sky had turned a cerulean blue and a slight breeze off the ocean skimmed the sweat from his skin.

He could think of worse assignments.

She, too, seemed to relax as the boat pulled away from shore, cutting across the nearly translucent blue swatch of water between Cancun and Isla Mujeres.

"I have to admit, the good part about my job is the freedom to choose my own schedule. And take off when I need to. And I needed this."

Yes, maybe he did, too. An assignment away from the cramped, cold quarters of his Prague apartment. He could already feel the sun baking his bones, uncoiling the tension of the past year. Years, actually.

"I don't want to walk into any surprises. Is there anything you need to know about me?" he asked. "We should make sure we look like an actual couple by the time we get there."

Although she'd put on her sunglasses, he saw her eyes widen. "I thought we'd ironed this out. I don't need your help."

"That came through loud and clear, but since I'm here, for the sake of world peace, let's work together."

She leaned over, pulled her feet out of her boots and took off her socks. She had cute toes with pink painted nails, a do-it-yourself job. "I guess you're right. We're all fixed up—it would spare us complications. Fine, you can be my date."

Awesome. Except her tone might make a guy just

throw himself overboard. Still, he tried a smile, just to be neighborly. "I promise to be the best wedding date you've ever had."

She pulled down her glasses and narrowed her eyes at him, as if she might be trying to see through him. "Really, I meant it about the nub thing. Just because I'll let you dance with me doesn't mean—"

"Got it, Scarlett. Just enough to be believable."

She pulled off her glasses and sighed. Then she shook her head. "I don't know what you heard, Luke, and truthfully, any other girl might be flattered by your dedication. But I'm just here for the wedding, and I'd like to see it go off without a hitch."

"Agreed."

She smiled, nodded and replaced her glasses. "Good. Everyone just needs to calm down." She pulled out a cap, put it over her hair and lifted her face back to the sun. "Everything is going to be just fine."

Right. Luke folded his arms over his chest, closing his eyes. Just fine. "I trust you," he said. What choice did he have?

TWO

"I don't know, Chet, there's something about Scarlett—er, Stacey. I don't think she likes me, for one. I clearly offended her."

"I think she thought that I expected a sort of, well, more *realistic* relationship. But the woman has more than a 'Keep Away' sign around her neck. She's wired with a thousand volts of don't-touch-me. And talk about cold. I think the Sanchez family is going to see right through us," he said into his international cell phone.

Luke sat on the edge of the king-size bed, watching the surf pound the reef, spit froth into the air and break on the coral outside his Lost Breezes cottage. He had taken off his shoes, letting the tile cool his feet, and in a second, he fully planned on jumping in the shower and washing off the sweat of the sun, the saline of the ocean and the still-stinging reception of Miss Hot-Around-the-Collar.

Scarlett had barely spoken to him the rest of the ferry ride, or even as they'd hailed another cab to the far end of Isla Mujeres, the Isle of Women, where the resort of Lost Breezes sat on the northern tip. He picked up a towel folded in the shape of a swan sitting on his bed, shook it out and rubbed it over his forehead.

"Staccy is from the private sector, but she came highly recommended by my pal David Curtiss. He mentioned that she was a lone wolf, but she said she was very capable and knows what she's doing."

Luke pictured Chet in his office in the Czech Republic, staring out at the snow along the Charles Bridge in Prague.

"So, you've never met her?"

"Just on the phone. But I'm confident she can handle herself. She probably *is* used to working alone, but this is a couple's job, so you need to get her to warm up to you."

"Believe me, no matter what I said, it was the wrong thing. It felt pretty chilly over on the port side of the ferry."

"Listen, Luke. If Sanchez's men think you're anything other than Lucia's special guests for her wedding, they'll take you out into the middle of the ocean and leave you for the sharks. Lucia has been working too hard and too long for this mission to go south."

"Scarlett's probably right. I could get the job done better solo, too."

"No, you couldn't. You need Stacey to act as Lucia's bridesmaid and your fiancée, otherwise you won't be able to stay close enough to Lucia to get her out of there when the CIA moves in on the Sanchez family. This mission all hinges on Lucia walking down the aisle on Saturday night. Augusto Sanchez will come out of hiding, and the CIA will finally get their hands on one of Panama's biggest crime bosses. We need you on-site, watching Lucia, or she could get killed. And she needs someone there to remind her that she's not in this alone. That's Stacey's job. Lucia's already had one scare."

"I thought you told me the accident in the market wasn't an attempted assassination."

"The CIA said it wasn't. But that's why she called for help. She's scared, Luke, and you gotta keep her calm. Focused."

Everyone just needs to calm down. Scarlett's words made a little sense now.

Luke stood up and leaned against the doorjamb that led out to the balcony. The salt weighed the air, layered his skin in grit. "And why, exactly, did Lucia call you?"

He heard Chet sigh. "We met in D.C. We're old friends."

Old friends. Luke didn't want to explore that meaning too far, but it was no wonder Chet didn't want to take this job. After all, Chet was recently married and he didn't need any reminders of past liaisons. Luke knew what ghosts could do to a guy—suck him back to the past, into his mistakes. No, Chet deserved a fresh start with his bride, Stryker International pilot Mae Lund. Luke's silence pushed Chet into confession.

"We may have had some sparks, Luke, but mostly, we were just friends. She was just a young law student, and I was in and out of the country with Delta Force. It wouldn't have worked. However, I also know Benito— her fiancé—from my Delta days, and if I showed up, he'd know Lucia had been betraying him, romantically and possibly otherwise."

"Chet, is Lucia expecting *you?*" Perfect, just perfect. At least he now knew what *not* to say.

"No. She's expecting one of my men. My capable, get-the-job-done-despite-personal-feelings men. That's you, Luke. But you might have to do more than just your job here, Luke. The Sanchez family has to believe that you and Stacey—"

"Scarlett."

"—are a couple, at least in public. So turn on some charm or something. You're good with the ladies—or at least you were. Dig deep and find that old lady-killer."

Luke walked through the bedroom to the tiny cement bathroom, turned on the faucet then stared into the mirror. He needed a shave. "I'm not that good, Chet. And besides, I'm not the guy I was."

He hadn't been that guy since he woke up one day to angry pounding on his hotel room door, looked at the woman on the other side of the bed and realized he'd turned into his lying, cheating father. Only Luke's lying and cheating hadn't exactly been his fault. Not that it mattered, in the end.

Chet's voice softened. "No, you're not. I know that."

"Besides, this girl isn't going to be charmed. She's a straight shooter, and she's not into playing games."

"So be the new guy—the gentleman."

The gentleman. He hadn't had much practice in that arena, either. Last time he had a date, the previous president had been in office.

"Most of all, get the job done. Keep Lucia and Stacey, for that matter—alive. No matter what it takes."

"Okay, boss." Luke said goodbye and hung up. Then he picked up the note left for him at the check-in desk. His "fiancée" hadn't stuck around long enough to read it with him, and of course, she'd booked her own solo accommodations.

Not that he expected to share. But in today's world, it might make convincing the Sanchez clan they were a couple just a smidge easier.

But perhaps this was for the best, because, just for a second, sitting beside her on the boat, watching her purse those unpainted lips that made her appear more innocent girl than hired muscle, well, he'd felt something shift inside. Add that to the way, for a second, she seemed even hurt, and yes, she'd unglued him long enough for him to wish he could take back his words in the cab—the ones that had put the pain in her eyes.

He went to the sink, washed his hands, pressed a towel to his face.

Stared at the familiar villain in the mirror.

Yes, he would turn on the charm, but only for the sake of the mission.

Three days was going to feel like eternity.

He opened the note and found a hand-scrawled script. *"Meet us on the boat by five for drinks and dinner. Lucia."*

Unfortunately, by the time they'd arrived, the cocktail hour had come and gone. Thankfully, he'd found out Scarlett's room number after greasing the palm of a valet in the lobby, one who had seen them enter the hotel together. It never hurt to make friends with the staff, and Raoul looked like a guy Luke might need later, so he added a retainer to his information gratuity.

And, with the twilight already hovering over the sea, Raoul had found a boat willing to skipper them out to the yacht.

Yes, the fun was about to begin.

Now these were the accommodations she'd hoped for—an ocean view, the sound of the seabirds, the briny redolence of the ocean. She loved it all, just as she knew she would. Not that she'd ever been to the sea before, but she'd read about it plenty of times in the romance novels that lined her shelves. And everything she'd read about Mexico and Isla Mujeres had told her she'd love it.

And to think she'd nearly missed all this.

Never again, champagne.

And while she was at it, she should probably calm down about her sister fixing her up again. Luke certainly wasn't a cretin. It could be much, much worse. Her sister might have found her a mechanic from Des Moines. Yes, it was possible that she'd ever so slightly overreacted to being paired with one of her sister's cast-offs. She wished he hadn't mentioned that he'd been "around the block" a few times, however. What, was that supposed to remind her that he was slumming with her?

For a second, the image of him leaning over a plate of sushi with her sister in some high-rise restaurant, the lights of New York City twinkling like starlight, shot into her brain.

Yes, perhaps he was simply reminding himself that normally his dates had a tan and wore less on their trips to Mexico.

She didn't want to know.

I really do know what I'm doing.

She just bet he did. But not with her, thanks.

I'm not just here to watch.

She'd nearly run from the cab, screaming. Really, she didn't even know where to start with her shakedown of Bridgett when she found her.

So much for calming down.

I'm here to do a job, same as you. A job? As if she was some sort of mission? *Befriend the bride's lumpy sister—someone has to do it.*

It hurt more than she'd imagined, and frankly, he

could have started out with a little charm, even if he'd had to fake it.

In fact, if he had led with something sweet, she might not have been so militant about going stag.

She shook Luke's arrogant words away. It seemed she'd set him straight after her comments on the ferry, however. He'd behaved himself after that.

Still, a girl didn't have to have it pointed out to her that Luke, her *non*date, might have been a good catch in other circumstances, with his wind-tousled golden-brown hair, brown eyes, the hint of fresh sun bronzing his skin as he considered her this afternoon.

I don't want to walk into any surprises. Is there anything you need to know about me?

Just what had Bridgett told him? *My pitiful sister— she's a temp, you know, has been for nearly ten years— needs a date for the wedding. Do you know she actually thought my fiancé was in love with her?*

Scarlett winced as she imagined Bridgett's voice. Nope, she didn't care how dedicated the man was, didn't care that Bridgett had flown him in. A girl had to stand up for herself, be her own hero. She didn't need Mr. Plus-One, thank you very much.

In fact, given the chance, she might have just found a plus-one on her own.

But when Luke had said something about looking like an "actual couple," it hit her.

It would be *easier* for everyone if she had a date. Her standing alone on the edge of the dance floor would only make everyone feel bad. If only her parents were alive, maybe it would be easier to be in Bridgett's shadow again. But it was just her standing at the sidelines. And, she didn't know what history Luke had, but he seemed to need to be her date.

Maybe he'd been in love with Bridgett. Wouldn't that be fun? She and Luke could stand together in the shadows and watch the bride and groom dance.

Maybe he was just what she needed. A guy who didn't expect anything, who just needed someone to stand next to when the lights dimmed. Yes, they could work together.

And she didn't want to make trouble, not again. So yes, she would pretend, for Bridgett's sake.

She'd simply ignore the fact that for a second—a long second—after he'd picked up her bag and carried it all the way to the top deck, after he'd settled on the bench beside her and the sea breeze had carried his strong and spicy scent, after he'd spoken to her in soft, almost gentle tones, she'd wanted him to *really* be her date.

Thankfully, she wasn't so foolish to think he was actually interested.

After all, she had learned her lesson with Duncan. A smart girl would have realized that in the two years Duncan spent being her friend, meeting her for coffee and learning to ballroom dance with her, he'd never once looked at her the way he looked at Bridgett, her beautiful sister, when she walked through the doors of the church.

Fresh off the runways of Milan, burnt out and needing a vacation.

In fact, no one *ever* looked at Scarlett the way they looked at Bridgett—not even their parents—but she thought she'd become used to that.

Until Duncan did it.

Yes, she knew what it felt like to be an afterthought, to disappear. So maybe she'd even enjoy having a man as handsome as Luke on her arm, even if it wasn't for real. Bridgett would be thrilled if Scarlett showed up on Luke's arm, her smile tucked into place. And this weekend was all about Bridgett, right? Besides, she could enjoy pretending, as long as she knew it was just a game. She'd been a theater major, after all.

Thankfully, the charade didn't have to start until tomorrow, according to the note her sister had left in her room inviting her to the dinner cruise, which she'd already missed. Scarlett left her a voice mail message in case her absence worried Bridgett.

She wouldn't hold her breath.

She stood on the balcony of her cottage, watching the sea hit the reef, break into a thousand shimmering pieces and crash onto the rocks.

She knew how that felt, to shatter into so many pieces you couldn't find them all. It happened the day Bridgett showed up on Duncan's arm to the church singles group. And the day she told Scarlett that she "just might stick around Rochester."

Duncan is a dentist! Scarlett wanted to scream as Bridgett climbed into her BMW, leaving her standing in the parking lot beside her rusty Sunbird. But Bridgett probably already knew that, because she introduced him to their Aunt Gretchen as Dr. Browne.

And then came the day when Bridgett moved off Scarlett's sofa and found her own condo.

Just over six months later, she and Duncan announced their engagement.

A seagull cried, dipping into the ocean for a morsel.

Scarlett should probably breathe in these few moments of peace before Bridgett and her bridal party—the ones who the bride really wanted to attend—returned.

If she'd had Bridgett's wedding dress in her possession, she might be tempted to simply hang it on her sister's door and take the midnight ferry back to the mainland. Bridgett didn't really want *her* anyway—just her organizational services. Scarlett replayed the voice mail in her mind. *Scarlett, my new maid of honor broke her leg in Vail. She can't attend the wedding. Is there any way you could fill in?*

Her *new* maid of honor. Scarlett had been the old maid of honor—with the big mouth.

There is so much left to do—organize the bachelorette day and bring my dress and the maid-of-honor dress, not to mention work with the wedding planner at the resort. Besides, I'm sorry. Really, I want you there. Please come.

Really. Scarlett must have been some sort of chump to call her back for details, let alone say yes.

Sure, Bridgett, I'll be glad to help. Let me just board my cat, take a leave of absence, drive to Minneapolis in a blizzard to pick up your dress and while I'm at it, maybe I can also plan your honeymoon—

Everyone just needs to calm down. Her own words. She breathed them in as she stood at her balcony in the warm air. She could get used to the ocean, so many shades of blue. On the ferry, she'd watched the mainland shrink, turning her gaze to the ocean floor as it slid by. The coral reefs, ledges and ripples seemed so close she wanted to dip her feet in. She'd pushed up her sleeves, letting her white skin see the sun for the first time in months.

She'd get a tan here, no matter what it took.

Sitting on the bed, she toed off her Uggs. The tile floor cooled her boiling feet. She probably needed a nap.

Or a shower.

She picked up the cute towel swan on her bed, holding

it in her hand. She could get used to this place. Maybe she could find a job here—after all, after ten years of temping, she knew how to fit in, make things happen quickly.

A skill, apparently, that had netted her this fun-filled weekend.

And no matter what anyone else said, she wouldn't call her reluctance to get a "real" job an inability to commit. She just liked change, that was all. And, well, she'd never found the one thing that she truly loved to do.

The shower cleaned from her the grime of the last sixteen hours. She found a blue sundress, one she'd worn maybe once and grabbed in a hurry, crumpled at the bottom of her carry-on. Maybe she could order room service. Or better, she'd venture out, under the glow of the stars, to the all-inclusive seafood dinner at the cabana. Then she'd park herself under one of those grass-covered umbrellas by the shore, under a tiki lamp, and lose herself in a book. Again.

She didn't even want to think about what Luke, her overachieving plus-one, might be doing.

Off her balcony, twilight had just begun to darken the ocean to an inky blue. Unseen seagulls cried against the surf. The smell of the sea drifted inside.

A night made for romance. Of course, her novel was the only romance she could count on. Not that she really *wanted* romance, but wouldn't it be nice if she could have a happily-ever-after? With a real-life hero, the kind she might find in her novel? Someone charming and strong, who saw her for the girl she wanted to be—if she could ever figure who that was?

The sultry air had clearly overheated her brain.

She put on a little makeup and was tying up her still-damp hair when she heard the knock.

Maybe Bridgett had returned and gotten her message.

As she opened the door her breath stopped, right there, caught in her chest.

So. Luke didn't play fair.

He stood under the glow of her porch light, looking freshly showered, his burnished golden-brown hair still wet, clean shaven and wearing a pair of black dress pants and a white silk shirt open at the neck. And he even smelled good.

"What?" Oh, she had a nicer side, really. She softened her tone. "Sorry I mean, can I help you?"

He grinned, as if she should be expecting him. "Hey. I know you probably thought we weren't on for tonight, but I got a note from the bride. She wants us to meet her on the boat."

"She does? I called and left her a message—the cruise already left."

"I know, but I found us a ride out to the yacht." He held out his arm. "Would you be so kind as to accompany me to dinner, Miss Scarlett?"

THREE

Scarlett sat in the back of the motorboat Luke had hired to take them out to sea, his words lingering like a song she couldn't get out of her mind.

Would you be so kind as to accompany me to dinner, Miss Scarlett?

He'd turned on the charm, and for a second there, she'd just about let his voice go right to her head.

Yes, Luke. Thank you. Had she really taken his arm? She'd walked an entire ten feet before she came to her senses.

This wasn't a date. She wasn't living in her romance novel, having met a mysterious man at a destination wedding who would sweep her off her feet and into a new life.

Instead, this was the man her sister had finagled into wooing her for the weekend, a man who had no real interest in her. After three days her name would stir nothing more than indigestion, so she'd better keep that in the forefront of her brain.

A game. She was just playing a game.

Sometimes her ability to fling herself into her fantasies just made her want to roll her eyes.

She turned into the wind. Her hair lashed her cheeks

in the salty air, and although she huddled in her ski jacket—she didn't care that she looked like a frumpy Minnesotan—her bare legs had turned to blocks of ice. Her sister had better be happy to see her after all this.

Luke sat across from her, outlined by the moonlight as the boat motored through waves toward the sprinkling of yacht lights in the distance.

Admittedly, he'd won this round. Not only had she taken his proffered arm, but she'd had no words to rebuff him, because he had gone to the trouble of getting her to her sister's dinner party.

As if he might be a bona fide gentleman.

"Why did she leave you a note and not me?" she shouted above the sound of the motor.

"Maybe she did. You were in a big hurry to get to your room." He grinned.

She yanked a thick chunk of hair from where it had lodged in her mouth.

"You look nice tonight, by the way." Luke's voice lifted above the motor's roar, and she glanced at him. He nodded too enthusiastically, like her response to his invitation had gone to his head.

Not a date. Not a date. "You, too."

The lights began to take form, and as the yacht came into view, Scarlett had to admit that international modeling must pay pretty well. The yacht resembled a small cruise ship, with three brightly lit decks rising from the sea to an observation deck…and was that a helicopter? Talk about overkill. But Bridgett never did anything in a small way.

No wonder Duncan fell so easily for her—no, that wasn't fair. Duncan happened to be a great guy, a man of faith and principles. He wasn't marrying her sister for her money.

Or her beauty.

But was she marrying him because he was some safe rebound after her race-car driving or soccer-playing boyfriends?

Scarlett glanced at Luke, suddenly glad that she didn't have to walk into dinner alone.

Coward.

Oh, yes. She even found a smile for Luke as the boat eased up to the stern of the yacht where they could disembark onto the deck. The motorboat seemed a toy next to the hulking ship. Two deckhands—bull-size men with the look of the sea about them—held the boat as Luke stepped out. He pulled her up behind him.

"Here we go," he whispered as he helped her up the steps onto the aft deck.

A little too much help, if anyone asked her, but she let him keep his hand on the small of her back anyway, just because the bigger of the two men stopped them, holding a metal detector.

And in his waistband…was that a gun? She glanced at Luke. To her surprise, he held up his hands.

Then the deckhand stepped forward and wanded him. Luke just let him, as if this might be something he expected.

Then the man stepped over to her and motioned for her to remove her jacket.

"What is this?" She backed away but Luke shook his head ever so slightly.

What on earth?

She glared at the man as Luke helped her slip off her jacket, then stood back as the man ran the wand over her, too. C'mon, it wasn't as though she could hide anything in a dress with spaghetti straps. The whole process made her feel dirty.

And even a little betrayed by Luke, who settled the jacket back over her shoulders and reached for her hand. But how pitiful had she become that she practically leaped when he offered it? Yes, she was a coward.

He pulled her close and curled her against him. "I know I don't need to say this, but you're truly a professional."

She had never been more offended in her life. Who, exactly, did he think she was? Just wait until she found Bridgett.

She heard the party going on somewhere in front of them, laughter drifting down from the deck above. She'd never been on a boat this size, however, and she took her time walking along the side deck, watching the lights splash on the dark ocean, getting her sea legs.

"This must have cost a fortune," she murmured.

"I think the family can afford it," Luke said, still holding her hand, walking in front of her.

"No, really, I don't think they can."

He glanced back at her, the slightest frown on his face. They emerged on the bow of the yacht where a band played steel drums, filling the night with a tropical beat. A couple of waiters held trays of pretty drinks and dark-haired women in dresses that certainly wouldn't have needed the wand danced together while men lounged on the chairs, laughing and smoking cigars.

Uh, maybe there was more than one wedding party on this ship. "She's not here. I think we have the wrong group," Scarlett said into Luke's ear.

She didn't let go of his hand, however. And bless him, he didn't let go of hers, either. See, he was a gentleman after all. She might decide to like him, just for now, despite the coerced dating.

He stopped a waiter and asked him something in

Spanish. She tried to catch it but he had a much better grasp of the language than she did, clearly, because he talked so quickly she got nothing. The waiter gestured up another deck.

"She's in her stateroom waiting for us," Luke said and pulled her toward the stairs.

Stateroom?

They found another group partying on the deck above. Not a familiar face here, either. She let Luke drag her to the back of the boat.

As he knocked on the stateroom door, she turned and stood for a moment, staring out at the mysterious black sea, the stars pinpricks on the undulating surface. The music, the flicker of lightning in the distance, the low tremble of thunder—she had entered a different world. "I can't believe Bridgett rented this. I mean, she's normally over the top, but—"

"What?" Luke sidled up beside her just as the door opened.

Scarlett turned, expecting Bridgett. Instead, a woman with dark hair, wide brown eyes and very red lips stood in the doorway. She was petite, beautiful and wearing an off-white silk gown that left nearly nothing to the imagination.

The woman glanced at Luke, then her gaze landed on Scarlett. What looked frighteningly like relief crossed her face.

"Finally," she said. Then she reached out and put her arms around Scarlett, hugging her as if she might be her long-lost friend. "I'm so glad you're here."

Something didn't feel right. Luke couldn't put his finger on it, but ever since they boarded the yacht—from the panic on her face when Sanchez's men wanded her, to her more-than-friendly grip on his hand, to the way her eyes widened when Lucia threw her arms around her—something about Scarlett seemed off.

She had been briefed, right? And it seemed that when she'd slid her hand onto his arm back at the resort, she'd even settled into their charade, had put on her game face.

Lucia grabbed Scarlett's hand and pulled her inside.

Luke followed and shut the door behind them. Wow, the drug business paid well. His tiny flat in Prague that he shared with Brody Wickham—he might be displaced soon, thanks to Brody's recent engagement to pop sensation Vonya—would fit three times over in Lucia's living room alone. Closed doors probably led to a bedroom and more. The place looked as if it should be in a showroom or a catalogue—a seafoam-blue sofa and overstuffed chair, cherrywood end tables, a giant flat screen on which played a soccer game. Opulence purchased with drug money.

The lavish setting probably accounted for Scarlett's wide-eyed look, which she cast first at Luke, then back at Lucia.

He tried to dismiss this sense that something wasn't quite right.

"I don't understand," Scarlett said softly.

Nope, there was no ignoring it any longer. Especially after Scarlett let go of his hand and said to the bride, the woman she'd been hired to protect, "Who are you?"

Who are you?

"This is Lucia, Scarlett. Lucia…the bride?" Luke said as calmly as he could.

Scarlett put a hand on his shoulder and pushed him back, her voice low. The wild look in her eyes—something between panic and fury, only tightened the knot in his gut. "I know the bride. This is *not* her. And I'm starting to wonder exactly who *you* are."

"I'm your…fiancé?"

She went white, put her hand to her chest, swallowed and stepped away from him. "Okay, *what* is going on here?" She took another step back toward the door, and Luke had no choice but to cut her off.

"Stop." He put his hand up and she flinched.

Oh, man. The sudden flare of fear in her eyes made him feel awful. "Listen, you are Stacey Meyer, right? From Denver? You know, my *bride-to-be?*"

After seeing the look on her face, he didn't know who to feel more sorry for—her, or himself. Because clearly he'd come to the wedding with the wrong date.

She drew in a breath, glanced at Lucia and then back at him. "My name is Scarlett Hanson, and I'm here for my sister Bridgett's wedding." Her voice had a sort of high twang to it. "But I think maybe you didn't know that, did you?"

He looked at Lucia, who had frozen. Who, in fact, might not even be breathing. "Lucia, everything is going to be fine—"

"Who is this woman?" Lucia asked, her voice shaking.

"I picked her up at the airport. I thought she was my contact—"

"Picked me up? *Picked me up?* Oh…oh, you listen here—whoever you are. You were in *my* cab, thank you very much, and you were supposed to be *my* date, not the other way around, so let's just rethink who picked who up, shall we?"

Perfect. He could spot a woman—no, women—about to unravel.

Oh, how he hated working with people he didn't know. It made it very easy for things to go wrong. Things like this.

"Ladies, please, let's just figure this out." He held up his hands in surrender to Scarlett. "Please, sit down. Let's talk about this."

Scarlett stood there looking at Luke as if he had spoken Russian. Then, she drew in a long breath and shuffled over to the sofa. She sat on the arm, her hands tangled together in a whitened grip. "Is your name really Luke?"

"Yes. And I'm assuming you are really Scarlett Hanson?"

"Always have been. From the moment I got into the cab with you."

Suddenly it all clicked—why she'd been so cold, even offended, when he'd suggested they might be a couple. And why she'd made sure he knew to keep his hands to himself. Oops.

He looked at Lucia and motioned for her to sit down. She shook her head.

Yes, next time he would definitely work solo. He schooled his voice into something resembling calm, hoping it might help him, too.

"Uh, okay, here's what's going down, Scarlett. Unfortunately, I was supposed to meet a woman named Stacey. She was my cover—my *fiancée*—for this mission. Clearly something happened to her."

"Mission?"

"I'm…well, let's just say I'm a security specialist. And in this case, I'm here to protect Lucia." He nodded toward her.

"Why does Lucia need protecting?"

"Because I'm marrying Benito Sanchez," Lucia said,

none too politely. She finally sat down in the overstuffed chair. "And someone is trying to stop me."

"Someone is trying to keep you from getting married?"

Lucia fiddled with the two-carat ring on her finger. Luke suddenly realized he should have noticed that Scarlett wasn't wearing a ring. Mistakes—how he hated them.

"Yes. Maybe because they've figured out that I'm not really here to get married," Lucia said.

"You're not?"

She lowered her voice, glancing at Luke as if for permission. Scarlett glared at him. He nodded. Scarlett deserved some information at this point. It was the least he could do.

"I'm here to help the CIA catch Augusto Sanchez. He's a terrorist and the leader of a drug and human trafficking cartel in Panama."

"I don't understand."

"Augusto is a shadow. Very few people actually know what he looks like, or where he lives. But he's my fiancé's uncle and he's coming to our wedding. The CIA will raid the wedding and arrest him."

"On your wedding day?"

"Well, I'm not really getting married, obviously." She cupped her hand over her mouth, swallowing, and Luke could see her tear. "Poor Benito." She closed her eyes and took a breath.

Scarlett just stared at her, horror on her face.

Luke even felt a little sorry for Lucia.

But that's what happened when you fell in love with liars. You got dirty, and people got hurt.

Lucia finally exhaled. "The problem is, I think someone knows the truth. Last week when I was at the market, someone tried to run me down, I know it." She lifted her arm, and Luke winced at the ugly scrape that reddened her skin. "I told my contact at the CIA but he didn't believe me. Frankly, I don't know who to trust, so I called a friend."

"My boss," Luke said quietly, trying to read Scarlett's face.

Scarlett turned to him and said, "So, this Stacey is supposed to be here protecting Lucia?"

"Yes."

"As a bridesmaid."

"Maid of honor. My friend from college," Lucia said.

"And if you aren't protected—"

"Then someone is going to kill me."

Scarlett looked at Luke and shook her head. "I'm an idiot."

"No, you're not."

"Oh, yes, I am. I should have known that a guy like you wouldn't be my date. I don't know where my head was."

Now what was that supposed to mean?

She stood up before he could ask. "Listen, Lucia, I am really sorry about messing things up here. And I pray you'll be safe." She turned to Luke. "Take me back to the island and I'll get out of your hair. You can track down this Stacey girl and get back to your mission." She held out her hand to Lucia. "Nice to meet you."

Lucia didn't move. She looked at Luke, her eyes glued to him.

Luke blew out a long breath.

Scarlett lowered her hand. "What's the problem?"

"Uh…Scarlett, I really don't know how to tell you this but, see, you went through security with me. And…"

Wow, he needed a drink—possibly more than water. Although those days were over, too. He sighed.

"Luke—"

"You can't leave." Lucia found her feet. "If Luke takes you back to the island and returns alone, they'll know something is up."

"What? No." She'd gone white, and he grimaced as he delivered her fate.

"She's right, Scarlett. You might not be Stacey Meyer, but you *are* my fiancée. At least for the next three days."

"My sister needs me. I can't stay here. She's expecting me to help her with her wedding—I have to pick up her dress!" Her voice shrilled as she lunged for the door.

Luke hated himself just a little when he caught her, his hands closing around her arms. And he felt even worse when he went all military on her, dropping his voice. "Scarlett. I absolutely cannot let you walk out of here."

FOUR

If this was a romance novel, she wanted to turn the page.

Go to the next chapter.

Maybe throw the book against the wall.

"Scarlett—"

"Stay away from me, whoever you are!" Scarlett pressed her hands against the walnut door of Lucia's bathroom, a room that just might be larger than her entire one bedroom apartment back in Minnesota. Definitely nicer, with the oversize soaking tub, the blue-veined marble vanity, the mirrored wall that only accentuated her distress.

She couldn't look at the fool in the mirror one more moment. So she turned against the door, slid down to the cool tile floor and rested her head on her knees.

"My name really is Luke," the voice said on the other side, softer now. She imagined him sitting on the floor also. His voice came right through the crack, right into her ear. "Luke Dekker."

A kind, even soft voice. Not at all like the voice that had slipped a knife of fear right through her, cold and steely and lethal just moments earlier. "You have to know that I truly thought you were my contact, Scarlett, or I would have never gotten into the cab with you."

"I got in the cab with you."

Silence. "What I mean is, I'm sorry that I assumed you were…"

"A secret agent?" For the first time, she let those words out, slippery as they were on her tongue. A secret agent. "You really believed I was your contact? That I could pull off this mission, whatever it is?"

"Protecting Lucia, and…yes. Well, truthfully, I had a couple moments of hesitation, but you were so, well, cold on the taxi ride, with all your 'I have to work solo' comments, that, yes, okay? Yes. I thought you were her. I thought you were my contact. My partner on this op."

"Didn't you get a picture?"

"I did. But, well, it looked like you. Sort of. People change, especially for roles. She had your hair. And your bone structure. And it was a black and white—oh, for goodness' sake, let's all admit that I am an idiot."

Oh, sure, that made her feel all better. "Well, if it eases your pain at all, I thought you were the man my sister set me up with for the weekend." Although, if interrogated, she might admit that she'd had her doubts, too.

Simply put, Luke Dekker just didn't seem like the kind of guy who would say yes to being set up with Bridgett Hanson's kid sister. He seemed capable of landing his own dates, thank you. No, Luke Dekker had a sort of "Bond, James Bond" aura that should have tipped her off from the beginning.

This isn't my first time around the block. His words came at her now and she winced. To think she'd thought he'd been hitting on her.

She just might stay in the bathroom forever. Die here. The bathtub might make a good coffin.

"I suppose we should start over again," he said through the door. "I didn't mean to scare you back there. We can work this out."

She recognized the tone—the one he'd used at her villa door this evening, the one that contained such villainous charm, the one that had cajoled her into this desperate excursion.

No. Call her a fool—twice even—but she knew when to cut and run from a temp job. She stood up and opened the door. "We're not starting over. We're ending this little game, Luke. Once again, take me home."

He had both hands bracketed on the frame of the door. She didn't know what she'd been thinking—that he'd simply shrug and say, "Sure honey, let me rev up the boat"? Because after one look at his expression, she went to slam the door shut again.

He caught it with his hand and used the other to push it back, to shove his way inside.

"Get out!"

"We went over this. I can't do that, Scarlett. They probably took your picture. They know you're my date—my fiancée. We're in this too far."

She backed up, reaching for anything. Her hand landed on the blue ceramic soap dish. She held it above her head and he stared at her as if she had contracted malaria. "For crying out loud, I'm not going to hurt you."

She looked at the soap dish, then back at him. He didn't seem menacing. Just a guy standing on a plush, blue bathroom carpet, his hands now in his pockets, as if trying to keep her calm. He didn't even look like an operative, special forces or whatever he might be.

Okay, sure, he had some decent shoulders, and those arms—fine, he probably worked out regularly. Still, an operative should have a weapon of some sort. And couldn't he have just taken the door?

Not if he was trying to make friends.

She hung on to the soap dish.

He sighed and what looked like real disappointment crested over his face. He reached out, showed her his hands, then sat on the side of the bathtub. "Let me tell you what is happening here."

Besides the ruin of her sister's wedding?

"That woman out there, Lucia, has put her life on the line for the past three years by dating Benito Sanchez. He's the youngest son of a guy named Claudio Sanchez, who just happens to be the brother of Augusto Sanchez. Augusto is a terrorist, among other things. If you'd like, I could get specific, but I don't think you need those images in your brain. Suffice it to say that he doesn't specialize. He's a drug lord and has a healthy stake in human trafficking on this side of the equator. The CIA and a few other three-letter organizations have been trying to lay their hands on him for years. But no one knows what he looks like, and he's painfully slippery."

He leaned forward, pressing his hands together as if he might be praying. "Lucia's roommate in college disappeared during a trip to Panama, and Lucia, who grew up in Brazil as the daughter of an American ambassador, found out that Augusto's organization was suspected in her murder. She had met Benito while in boarding school and decided to work with the CIA to see if she could wheedle her way into the Sanchez family. It's taken three years, but finally, we have a chance at catching him."

"I never thought Benito would ask me to marry him." Lucia slipped into the room, her hands wrapped around her tiny waist. "Or...that I'd fall in love with him." She gave a small, tight smile. "But the wedding gave us the perfect opportunity to ferret out Augusto. He loves Benito. He won't miss the wedding."

"And the CIA will be waiting for him on Saturday night, right before Lucia walks down the aisle."

Saturday night. "My sister gets married Saturday morning. We're having the reception on a yacht," Scarlett said.

"Good. Then she'll be long gone by the time the fun starts."

"And what happens to Lucia?" Scarlett set down the soap dish and looked at her.

"She leaves before they find out who betrayed them."

"And Benito?"

Lucia closed her eyes. Clearly, without Benito.

Scarlett didn't know who she felt sorrier for, Lucia or poor Benito, who thought Lucia loved him. Yes, poor Benito.

"It sounds like you have it all worked out." Scarlett's voice emerged with too much steel. She understood what it felt like to be on the receiving end of betrayal. "You don't need me."

"But we do need you." Luke stood up. "Like Lucia said, someone tried to kill her last week."

Scarlett glanced at Lucia, whose eyes had reddened. Lucia nodded. "I was in the market and a car slammed into a vendor's kiosk, nearly hitting me. The CIA thinks it was an accident, but someone in the Sanchez household has been following me." She glanced at Luke. "That's why I called Chet. I knew he would believe me."

"And I'm supposed to stop this person? I'm just a

temp. I file. Type. Arrange parties, sometimes. I hate to tell you this, double-oh-seven, but I'm not the girl you'd hoped for. My most lethal skill is my driving, I assure you."

This got the smallest of smirks from Luke, even as he shook his head. "That's why I'm here. To watch your back."

"So, what, I'm just supposed to—"

"Hang out with the bride. Let me know who's with her, and where she'll be, and when. Be her maid of honor."

The maid of honor. Oh, boy. "I'm already the maid of honor at my sister's wedding. And if I'm not there, she'll have a meltdown. If you think this guy Augusto is dangerous…"

Another smirk.

"I can't, Luke. Even if…" Even if she wanted to. Which she didn't. Right?

"They will make it look like an accident," Lucia said to Luke. "I think I'm safe in my stateroom. Benito is often here, and he has guards on the boat. Everyone aboard has been checked for weapons, so I think I only need protecting when I'm in public." She touched Luke's arm. "Maybe Scarlett's right. And if you're with me, I'm sure it will be okay," she said, sounding anything but sure.

Scarlett wasn't sure why Lucia's words tugged something inside her. Lucia clearly loved Benito and—

"I know you're right. The last thing I should do is involve a civilian," Luke said.

Yes, that made sense. But wait, she wasn't a complete idiot. How hard was it, anyway, to be Lucia's maid of honor, to make sure no one got too close to her? "I don't have to be with my sister every moment," she said before she could stop the words from slipping out.

Oops.

But really, the goons on the deck below did believe she had come with Luke. She couldn't walk out on the bride, could she?

But Luke had already decided. She saw it on his face. "We'll stage a fight and break up."

"What? No, I'm not getting into a fight with you."

"Why not? You're so good at it."

She narrowed her eyes at him.

"See?" But his grin was halfhearted. "I'll tell them we had a fight, or better, that you were seasick. That will at least keep you off the yacht."

"Fine. Whatever." But she couldn't help the disappointment. "Just...take me home."

Or rather, to the island.

Or...what? She didn't know what she wanted. She glimpsed herself in the mirror over the bathtub. She almost didn't know that woman—her dark hair windblown, shoulders bare, standing with her arms crossed over her chest, wearing a look of determination she didn't know she possessed.

In fact, she sort of looked like a secret agent.

"I'm sorry I got you into this mess, Scarlett. I'll make sure you get home safely."

Awesome.

She gritted her jaw as she brushed past Lucia, not looking at Luke. Picking up her jacket on the way out, she climbed down the stairs, gooseflesh raising on her legs.

The murky black of the ocean tossed the yacht, and she had to grab the rail as it pitched her off balance.

A warm hand pressed her back and she whirled around.

"Sorry." Luke withdrew his hand. *Touch me once and you'll pull away a nub,* she'd said.

Real nice, Scarlett.

She refused to grab his steadying hand as she made her way down the side of the boat, climbing down to the deck and, finally, holding down her skirt to maneuver onto the motorboat.

Luke climbed in beside her. "You okay?"

Her eyes burned. Maybe not, but she nodded, because she couldn't figure out why she wouldn't be.

They rode home, the motorboat cutting over the waves, slamming into the troughs, jarring her bones. Wrapping her jacket around her, she drew up her knees, trying not to shiver. The lights of the island sparkled on the waves, the stars overhead dusty across the sky. Luke sat in the front, sometimes turning to look at her.

Always with that stoic expression.

I'm sorry. The words lodged in her throat, because frankly, none of this was her fault.

Not really.

They pulled up to the dock. As she tried to find her balance, he rose, hopped to the dock, then reached out as if to pull her up.

She debated a moment then took his hand. His warm, strong hand. He pulled her to the dock.

In the darkness, with only the moonlight on his face, his eyes on hers, she suddenly didn't want to leave. Didn't want to slink back to her shadowed hut. Didn't want to wake up in the morning back in her own skin— Bridgett's unremarkable little sister.

"I can make it from here," she said.

He drew in a breath. "Again, I'm so sorry for the trouble. Have a good wedding."

"You, too."

"It's just a job."

That's right, it was. But it was one she, the temp, might have liked to try. The truth came at her fast, with the bite of regret. Yes, she might have wanted to see if she could save the day.

"Good night, Luke. Sorry you weren't my date."

He smiled. "Me, too. Good night, Scarlett."

And then, like the mystery he was, Luke climbed back into the boat and disappeared into the curtain of night.

Luke just wanted to keep going, lose himself in the black expanse of the ocean.

How could he have mistaken Scarlett Hanson for an operative? And then, even briefly, considered that she should take Stacey's place? That more than anything seemed proof that he'd lost function of his brain synapses.

He'd kept staring at her in the boat as they'd gone back to shore—not that he meant to, but disbelief kept him glancing back at her, huddled in the jacket, her eyes huge in the moonlight.

Chet would kill him.

And where was Stacey?

Even better—how was he supposed to keep Lucia safe? He'd have to stay on her like glue, but with Benito nearby and without a date for cover...

Yeah, that could get interesting.

He knew a little about how jealousy could warp a man's brain, turn him violent. The last thing he needed was Benito throwing him off the yacht for perceived wrong intentions.

The boat churned through the ocean, spray misting his face.

Sorry you weren't my date. For a second, on the pier, he'd nearly pressed his hand to her cheek, his heart giving the strangest leap at her goodbye, as if he actually hoped she'd stay.

And do what? Be his fiancée? No, this was better—now he could work alone, call the shots.

This was the best thing, for both of them. He hadn't exactly been looking forward to feigning romance, letting fake words roll from his lips, kissing a woman he didn't love.

It all felt way too much like what Darcy had done to him. Her name roiled something nauseous inside him. *You're married?*

No, he wouldn't go there. And besides, with Scarlett, the act would have been part of his job. Not a diversion from her life in the suburbs, like Darcy, a bored housewife from D.C.

He lifted his face to the wind, gritty and thick against his face. The lights of the yacht came into view. The music had died, the guests finding their berths or leaving. Maybe he could take up residence in Scarlett's berth. At least he could be on the yacht, available 24/7, keeping watch over Lucia. He'd give her a pager, something he'd planned to pass on to Scarlett.

He could do this. He'd simply say Scarlett had a severe bout of seasickness. And on the day of the wedding? He'd make it up as he went along.

Oh, how he hated mistakes.

The driver cut the engine as he pulled up to the yacht.

The same two goons who'd met him the first time helped him aboard. "Where's your girlfriend?"

He slid the lie out with a shrug and a look of impatience. One laughed, the other made a crude remark. But they allowed him back onto the yacht.

He averted his eyes from a couple locked in a late-night tryst on a lounge chair and climbed the stairs to Lucia's stateroom.

Lucia answered the door, her eyes wide, flashing warning, her tone sweet. "Oh…hello. I didn't expect you." She opened the door, motioning him in.

Really? But he'd told her he'd be returning—

Benito. Her fiancé sprawled on one of the white leather sofas, his silk shirt open, his linen pants wrinkled, his feet bare. He grinned drunkenly, his short dark hair windswept. *"Hola."*

"I got Scarlett home safely," he said to Lucia.

"How is her stomach?" She said it loud enough for Benito.

"Better, I think, but she may be sick the entire weekend. Sailing isn't for her."

"You—who are you?" Benito pushed himself off the sofa, came over and draped his arm over Lucia. "Do I know you?"

Lucia wore a stricken expression.

"I don't think we've met, pal," Luke said, holding out his hand.

Benito ignored it. "I did not invite you."

He glanced at Lucia. "Uh…no. Lucia did."

"She invited a strange man to our wedding?"

"I'm her maid of honor's fiancé." He hoped he sold the lie, because suddenly Benito didn't seem that drunk.

Sure enough, Benito's eyes narrowed. "Fiancé?"

"Remember, Benny, I told you about her. My housemate in college? She was here earlier but got sick. Luke ran her back to the mainland."

Benito caught her hand, turned his face into it and kissed it. "I think so. Stacey someone?"

Lucia gave a hard laugh. "No. No, Stacey was the other housemate—the one we wanted to kick out." She glanced at Luke. "Scarlett was the good one. Who liked pink?"

Benito smiled, nodding even as she leaned in tight to him. Clearly Lucia knew how to distract him. But he let go of her hand and turned to Luke.

"Why are you here without your fiancée?"

Good question, Benny. "I came back to pick up her dress. She needs it for the fitting tomorrow."

Lucia glanced at him with a flash of a smile. "Yes, it's in my closet. I'll retrieve it for you in the morning, but I think it's too late to return to the mainland, don't you, Benito? He can sleep here—"

"Here?"

She gave a laugh, and Luke hoped Benny was too drunk to notice the way her voice shook. "In the state-room next door. The one I reserved for her."

Benito pressed his hands against her cheeks. "Anything for you, *chiqua*." He rounded on Luke, his finger pointing but missing its target.

"My Lucia needs her maid of honor. You will get her," Benito said, getting some spittle on Luke. "Tomorrow. We will pick her up tomorrow." He pressed his finger into Luke's chest. "I want to meet your fiaaaancée."

Luke resisted the urge to smack his finger away, finding instead a smile. "If she's well."

Benito patted him on the cheek. "She'll be well." He pulled Lucia close. "Isn't my bride beautiful?"

Lucia looked up at Benito, something Luke couldn't place in her eyes.

"Yes, she is."

Benito's expression hardened. "Don't you look at her."

Luke slid his gaze back to Benito. Right. Okay. "Good night."

He met Lucia's eyes when Benito turned back to her. She gave him a slight nod. Clearly, despite Benito's intoxication, she believed she had nothing to fear.

Probably not, but he'd be right next door. Trying to figure out how to keep Scarlett away from the yacht. Maybe she could come down with a convenient case of malaria.

He let himself out of the room and closed the door. A man stood at the rail, his shirt whipping in the wind. He wore linen pants, not unlike Benito, his feet in sandals. A gold band on his right ring finger glinted in the moonlight.

"*Hola,*" he said, not looking at Luke. "A beautiful weekend for a wedding, no?"

Luke drew in a breath. Claudio Sanchez. He stepped up beside him. "Beautiful."

He stayed silent for a moment, the boat rocking with the rhythm of the waves. "I love the sea. The wind carries the souls of the lost. I can hear them sometimes, moaning."

Luke gripped the rail, staring out into the blackness. Yes, the ocean at night seemed fathomless, dangerous. Even haunted.

"This boat was a gift, you know. From an old friend."

"It's quite a gift."

"Yes. He and I grew up together in the same village. Our mothers were friends. Our fathers, too. Manuel was a lawyer, went to school in America while I scrabbled to make a living in Panama."

"You did well for yourself," Luke said.

Claudio slanted his gaze at him. He had a square, solid face, dark eyes that seemed to linger too long on Luke. His thick hands stayed at the rail. "Real estate. I bought my first apartment complex, a little place in our village, when I was eighteen. People always need a place to live."

Oh, Claudio lied well. To outward appearances, he was Panama's version of Donald Trump. Except no one would call The Donald a slumlord. Or worse, a conduit for his brother's trafficking businesses. Luke didn't even want to guess how many women and children Claudio owned, how many brothels he ran. Real estate, indeed.

"I finally convinced Manuel to move back to Panama, and I gave him a job. He was a good lawyer. Kept me out of the courts."

And what Manuel couldn't plea-bargain, Claudio probably took care of via other means.

"He grew quite wealthy."

"And bought you a yacht?"

Claudio lifted a shoulder. "It belonged to a competitor. Manuel helped me acquire it. We sat right down there," Claudio pointed to the deck, where the lovers had finished their tryst and the deck chair sat empty, "and toasted to our good fortune. I remember that night as if it were yesterday, the expression on my wife's beautiful face as she looked at him, her eyes shiny. She sat in my arms, toasting our fortune, and smiled at him. The little seductress."

Something inside Luke began to clench.

"I knew, of course, that they'd been together. Why

not? Esmeralda could steal a man's breath from his lungs, make him forget his name. His place."

He turned away from the deck, his back against the rail, folding his arms across his bullish chest. "I found them in the cabin next door." He gestured with a nod of his head. "They died slowly, dragging through the water off the end of the boat, their blood a trail for the sharks. Sometimes I can still hear their screams."

He glanced now at Luke. "I hope my son has a long and happy marriage." He sighed then clamped a hand on Luke's shoulder. "What was your name again?"

"Luke. Dekker."

"Nice to meet you, Luke." He turned back to the rail. "Did I see you come aboard with a beautiful woman?"

"You did, sir. My fiancée. She's Lucia's maid of honor. But I had to take her back to the mainland—seasickness."

"What a shame. I look forward to meeting her." He met Luke's eyes, smiled, then turned back to the darkness. "Yes, I do love the sea."

FIVE

No, thank you very much, Scarlett did not want to move from the villa near the sea to the single room on floor eleven of the Lost Breezes Hotel. But she would anyway.

"Let me just get my bags," Scarlett said, pushing her hair back from her face. The breeze tickled the gauzy drapes of the porch, now open to the reef. Outside, waves pounded the coral, the gulls crying into the morning.

"Again, ma'am, we're very sorry, but they double-booked your room. And since your reservation came in second, the other guests were given priority."

Of course they were. And of course, she'd packed up her belongings, following the valet as he lugged them across the crushed coral walkway back to the hotel, into the murky dampness of the hallway, up eleven stories to a room that overlooked the salt-sprayed town of Isla Mujeres, with its dirt alleyways and tiny cement homes in faded blue-and-pink paint, cast-iron balconies jutting from wooden windows. From here, she could make out the ferry launch on the other side of town with the two boats docked, ready to transport tourists back to the mainland.

If she kept going and hailed a cab, she could probably

make the nine o'clock ferry. Or—oh, ten! "Is it really ten o'clock? I think I forgot to change my watch," she asked, looking at her watch as she tipped the valet, a handsome man she'd guess to be nineteen with dark skin, big brown eyes, an eager smile.

"No, ma'am."

Phew.

"It's nearly eleven."

"It can't be, the time change can't be that much."

"It's the sea air. It makes everyone exhausted. But if you hurry, you can still make the breakfast buffet."

He backed out of the room and she sat on the bed, a white cotton blanket over the top, an elephant made of towels in the center. The place smelled of algae, too much time spent soggy, not enough in fresh air. Up here, the room didn't catch the same breezes as down by the sea.

Thanks, sis.

Then again, no one had known she was attending until three days ago.

But we do need you. She couldn't get Luke out of her head. She closed her eyes against the memory of his voice, but he only appeared in her mind as he had standing under the moonlight, something in his eyes that made her think he might actually miss her. *Good night, Scarlett.*

Oh, she had to push double-oh-seven out of her head and get her brain where it belonged—on Bridgett's wedding. That's why she'd come to this overbaked island—to help her sister marry the man of her dreams.

Or, once upon a time, Scarlett's dreams. Except maybe not, because the moment she'd sat down in the taxi, she realized she'd been aiming a bit too low.

That's right, for six whole hours, she'd been a secret

agent, or at least mistaken for one by a guy who actually protected people for a living. Top that, Duncan Browne.

Slipping on her sandals, she grabbed her room key, left her bags packed and walked down the hall to the elevators.

She scooted in next to an older couple, the woman in a broomstick skirt and a wide straw hat, the man in a pair of Bermuda shorts. "Are you here on vacation?" the woman asked.

"A wedding. My sister's."

"We're celebrating our fiftieth," the man said. "Gayle and Louis Bingham, from Michigan."

"Scarlett. I'm from Rochester."

"New York?"

"Minnesota." She smiled at them as she exited, fast-walking through the cool air of the hotel and outside into the bath of humidity. Her skin immediately felt clammy, but she'd take sea breezes over canned air any day.

Her hotel reservation came with the all-inclusive package—at least it had when she checked in—so she angled toward the straw-roofed cabana with the breakfast buffet.

She walked in, scanning the room, wishing for just a moment that she might see Luke. But he'd probably returned to the boat and long forgotten her.

She made her way to the end of the buffet table, picked up a plate and opened one of the stainless steel containers. Empty. The next one contained a blackened piece of bacon, and the next the gelled remnants of scrambled eggs. She took a spoonful, added the bacon. Gone were the eggs Benedict, the sausages, the crepes, the fried potatoes. She managed to score a cold piece of wheat toast, then turned, searching for her sister.

Sure enough, at five tables jammed together, her sister sat holding court with her two other bridesmaids— former models from her days overseas—and her three groomsmen. She chatted with them as she finished off a bowl of granola and yogurt.

Her sister, as usual, could eclipse every other person in the room with her creamy tanned skin, her long sun-streaked blond hair, that wide smile, those green eyes. That she'd inherited all the tall genes just didn't seem fair. Duncan sat next to her, his hand draped easily over the back of her chair, his eyes on her, shining. He looked as if he hadn't seen the sun in close to a decade until yesterday. His skin was lobster red down his nose, along his arms. Someone needed to up their SPF protection.

Or not. Let him fry.

"Hey, guys." Scarlett walked up to the table, finding a smile.

Bridgett had been laughing at something. Now she grabbed a napkin, pressing it to her mouth. "Oh, Scarlett, hi! When did you get here?"

So much for her sister sitting in some dark corner in the fetal position, paralyzed with worry. "Last night. I left a message on your phone."

"You did. Oh." She turned to Duncan. "Did you see a message on the phone?"

He didn't look at Scarlett. "No, sweetie," he said, kissing Bridgett on the nose.

Why eat? She'd just lose her breakfast.

"I'm so glad you made it." Bridgett stood, leaned over the table and gave her an air-kiss. "Where's my dress?"

Oh, the dress. The dress. "Uh…it's in good hands." Dress update…check.

"Thanks, sis. I knew you would take care of me. Join us. Everybody, make room for my kid sister." She waved her arms as people scooted their chairs down. A woman who looked as if she hadn't eaten this decade, her hair gathered high in a deliberately messy ponytail, reached out with her French manicure to grab a chair. She pulled it toward the corner of the table.

"Here you go, hon." She patted the wicker.

Perfect. Scarlett sat down.

"Is that all you're eating?" Bridgett said. "They have doughnuts up there." She turned to her group. "Scarlett has a standing order for a Danish at the bakery cart at church."

"This is all that was left," Scarlett said, picking up her blackened bacon. "But I'm not hungry."

"Oh, they had homemade crepes with raspberry sauce. So good," Bridgett said. "I had two!" She winked. "I'll probably have to starve the rest of the day. I hope they offer wraps for our spa day today." She looked at Scarlett, her waxed eyebrow high.

Scarlett took a drink of orange juice, hopefully one that didn't belong to someone else. Why was her sister looking at her like that?

"You did put together the spa day, right? You got my email?" Bridgett's smile dimmed and Scarlett had the faint memory of her sister mentioning a bachelorette day at the spa. But she'd taken that as an invite, not a directive to plan it. Still, how difficult could that be?

"Yes. Of course. And I'm pretty sure they have wraps."

"A seaweed wrap. You gotta try one, Scarlett. They're amazing. The seaweed seeps into your skin, and you can just feel your whole body coming alive."

One bachelorette party with a seaweed wrap, check.

"The girls are going into town to do some souvenir shopping. But we'll be back in time for lunch. I'm assuming we'll do the spa in the afternoon?" She turned to Duncan, who gazed at Bridgett with such adoration that Scarlett felt he could use a good slap to bring him back to reality.

"I'm so excited about our beach party tonight—shish kebabs on the beach. I can't wait." She leaned into his arms, looking at Scarlett. "You checked the menu, right? Remember, no mushrooms—oh! I'm so rude. Scarlett, this is Dylan, from Davenport. He has his own mechanic's garage, isn't that wonderful?" She looked at Scarlett and a person would have to be seated on the other side of the island not to have seen her gratuitous wink.

Dylan smiled at her. He was a nice-looking man the size of a bulldozer who'd given up on hair and went for the shaved-head look. "So, you fix cars?"

"Yep," Dylan said, reaching for her hand across the other two bridesmaids.

"And you're—"

"Duncan's cousin."

Of course he was. And then the gears clicked into place. Oh. Meet her *real* date for the weekend.

That seemed about right. See, this was her world—fetching wedding gowns and planning seaweed wraps and dancing with the beefy cousin of the groom. Not high-seas secret missions with devastatingly handsome men who spoke softly to her in the moonlight.

Oh, why hadn't she said yes to Luke?

"Gotta go, sis." As one, Bridgett and her two skinny bridesmaids rose from the table. "Hey, I don't want my bran muffin." Bridgett took the muffin and dropped it onto Scarlett's plate. "Why don't you have it? I know it's not a Danish, but…" She winked again.

If Scarlett ran, she could probably make the noon ferry.

Lucia was going to die and Luke right along with her if he didn't find Scarlett.

Lucia's scream sent him flying out of his bed in the early morning. He'd untangled himself from his covers, clad only in his dress pants, and lunged for the door, throwing it open just as Lucia opened her mouth again.

And no wonder.

Still thrashing on the decking outside her room, blood oozing from the speared hole in its gut, a reef shark fought for its last breath.

And Lucia had nearly tripped over it. Now, she pressed her hands to her mouth and turned her wide gaze to Luke.

He reached out, yanked her away from the bloody, thrashing mass and pulled her to himself. "Are you okay?"

She clung to him, nodding.

"What is this?" Benito stood at the door, bare-chested in a pair of boxers. He glanced at the dying shark, then at Luke.

Who released Lucia.

Benito's eyes narrowed. "What is going on?"

Lucia launched herself at Benito, wrapping her arms around his waist. "I found it when I came out—it scared me." She looked up at Benito and Luke had no problem believing her.

But Benito's eyes were glued to Luke. "What are you doing here?"

"I heard a scream...I just got here."

Benito's eyes narrowed for a moment, then he stared at the shark. It had stopped moving. "Where did this come from?"

"I don't know." Lucia still had her arms around Benito, holding on as if she meant it.

Benito nudged the animal with his toe. "Who would do this?" He looked at Luke.

Luke held up his hands. "I didn't hear anything."

Benito turned to Lucia, "You're trembling."

"I...it just surprised me."

"I'm sorry, Lucia. My family has many enemies, some who would not want me to marry an American." He pressed a kiss to her forehead. "Someone is on this boat who shouldn't be, and we will find them if we have to do a background search on every guest. You will be safe on our wedding day."

Luke glanced at Lucia. Could it be that Benito thought someone might be out to get *him?*

Benito turned to Luke. "Where is your woman?"

His—oh, Scarlett. "Back at the resort."

"Fetch her—I don't want Lucia to be alone today." He kissed her again, then pressed her inside their cabin. But his gaze stayed on Luke. "And you. Keep your hands to yourself."

Luke shoved his hands into his pockets. Benito shut the door.

Background checks would not be good. Sure, Luke's had been washed for this mission and Scarlett probably had the only clean background check out of all the guests on this yacht. But if Luke didn't get her information and get it to Artyom, Stryker International's techno-geek to wash and doctor, Benito would notice a giant hole in her resumé, the kind that didn't include having lived with Lucia.

Luke grabbed his shirt, slipped on his flip-flops and climbed down the stairs to the main deck.

"I need to get to the mainland," he said to one of the two watchdogs standing guard by the launch.

"We'll be there in an hour." He pressed his hand on Luke's chest. "You can wait."

You can wait.

Yeah, he'd waited, his stomach nearly inside out as the yacht motored to shore. He'd sat in the sun on the deck, prepping for his conversation with Scarlett, remembering the firm grip she'd had on the soap dish.

Like she might want to bean him with it.

Hey, Scarlett, remember me?

Oh, nice. Charming. As if she could forget him— well, maybe she could, but he certainly wouldn't forget her.

No, she'd been embedded in his brain for a good, long portion of last night, the way she watched him as he motored away, something like longing on her face.

He hadn't known what to do with the feelings that look churned up.

I know that we said we could probably handle this, that we didn't need you.

As far as ideas went, the one he was currently entertaining ranked as colossally bad. He'd been out in the sun too long if he believed that talking Scarlett into masquerading as Lucia's maid of honor—even as a companion with whom to sunbathe—might be a remotely reasonable option.

Only, Benito seemed pretty convinced that he had been today's shark target. And Scarlett, no doubt, had the background of Bambi, something that could work in their favor. *See, Lucia found a dead shark outside her room today, and she needs a friend.*

Yes, he could imagine Scarlett's face when he got to that part. And the part after it. *So, today, we'll need you to hang out on the yacht with Lucia and pretend to be her friend while they check our backgrounds. Oh, and be on the lookout for more sharks.*

Claudio's conversation hovered in the back of his mind. *Oh, how I love the sea.*

What if he just grabbed Lucia and made a run for it? It would dismantle three years of undercover work and alert the entire Sanchez clan, far and wide, and they'd make it as far as the Cancun airport.

I promise I won't let anything happen to you, Scarlett.

And then she'd look at him with those green eyes, disbelief in them, because he'd done an oh-so-stellar job of earning her trust thus far. He'd be lucky if she didn't try to slam the door in his face.

Or, on his foot, which he'd shove into the door to make sure that didn't happen.

Because, really, he did need her. At least for about six more hours, until he could figure out her airtight alibi explaining why she suddenly ditched the wedding of her best friend.

He wasn't above staging an all-out fight. A brilliant breakup in front of the entire Sanchez clan, preferably because he'd betrayed Scarlett with an onboard fling. However, that would most likely get *him* thrown off the boat.

No, he needed to make it seem as if *she* had done the betraying, because his getting kicked off the yacht wouldn't help anyone.

Especially Scarlett and Lucia.

Maybe he could make Lucia kick Scarlett off the boat. But what could make the bride oust her best friend from the wedding?

He could use a few ideas right now. He even lifted his face to the hot sun, as if he hoped heaven might be listening.

What was he thinking? God hadn't listened to him since the day he'd broken one of the Cardinal Rules.

Like, do not commit adultery.

Yeah, Luke might as well resign himself to the fact that God wasn't going to trust him again, thanks.

So, instead, he sat on the deck, wishing he'd brought his sunblock, hoping Scarlett would at least listen as he jammed his foot in her door and begged for a second chance.

The yacht finally docked at the far side of the resort, and Luke did his best not to run until he had rounded the side of the hotel. Then, he took off down the coral pathway to the villas.

He knocked on her door, putting his hand on the frame then removing it. Then putting it back.

The maid opened the door, holding a handful of towels. *"Si?"*

"I'm looking for the woman who is staying here. Is she around?"

"No, *señor,* she left."

"When will she be back?" As if the maid would know.

"No, no, *señor.* Left." The woman flipped to Spanish. "She took her bags and moved out."

"She left. Left?"

"Si, señor."

Left? Scarlett had left the island? But what about her sister's wedding?

Luke turned away from the door and walked out into the sun. Of course she left. Because that's what the people he really needed did in his life.

Because that's what he deserved.

SIX

"Why can't I have the coffee and chocolate wrap?" Scarlett stood on the wooden mat in the private room, her hands over her upper body while the spa technician applied, as one would butter, a paste of sea mud on her torso. The woman had already mudded her legs, wrapping them in plastic. Given one good push, she just might topple over. Now, she attacked Scarlett's stomach. Scarlett averted her eyes.

"Because this pulls the toxins out of your body. You'll be five pounds thinner, I promise." Bridgett lay on her back, staring at the ceiling after being slathered in yogurt.

The other two bridesmaids had moved on to Mayan massage and facials. Thankfully, Scarlett had started with a pedicure, her toes now a lovely passion pink, something that at least made her feel pretty while encased in mud.

And she might have forgone the mud wrap altogether if her sister hadn't hooked her by the arm, trotted her through the tiled hallways of Dream On Spa, with the aromatic smells, the rush of waterfalls, the piped-in harp music. Or perhaps that was live. Could be, since the spa cost a small fortune—or rather, cost Bridgett a small fortune, thanks to her handing over her credit card to Scarlett. But a woman who had a penthouse in New York and a chateau in France could probably afford to treat her bridesmaids to a little luxury, right?

"The wrap will help you get into the dress. Debbie was a bit less, well, hippy, than you are. So we had to take your dress in for her after…well, you know."

"Thank you for that reminder." Scarlett lifted her arms as the technician wound her in plastic wrap. "How many times do I have to apologize? I agree I shouldn't have had that champagne. It went right to my head."

"I've already forgiven you." Bridgett's plastic crinkled as she peeked out from one of the cucumber slices covering her eyelids. "Really." She gave Scarlett a smile that made the drying yogurt on her face crack. "Why do you think I set you up with Dylan?"

Payback? "I don't need a date, Bridge. Really. I can do just fine on my own."

Bridgett didn't move. "If you were doing just fine on your own, you would've never thought you and Duncan were actually an item. You made that relationship into more than it was because you're afraid of a real one."

Scarlett opened her mouth, but apparently Bridgett had more to say.

"You spend every night with your nose stuck in a novel, dreaming up some hero, when you should be going out and finding one in real life."

"I don't need a hero—"

"You know what I mean. A man. A real man, not a make-believe character."

"And that's Dylan?"

"He's Duncan's cousin. And yes, he's very nice."

"He has rough hands." Even as she said it, the memory of Luke's hand in hers swept through her mind, his strength as he'd led her across the yacht, as he'd helped her onto the dock. She closed her fists as the technician began to massage the mud onto her arms.

"Dylan has mechanic's hands. But he's very nice. Give him a chance."

"I wish you'd stop setting me up, Bridgett. I'm not a charity case."

Bridgett drew in a breath. "Maybe I just want to make sure you don't have any relapses."

Oh, why hadn't she taken the ferry? She could be sitting on an airplane right now.

No, why hadn't she simply agreed to help Luke last night? Agreed to watch Lucia's back? How hard could it have been? And maybe, for once, she'd actually live the romance novel instead of just read it. Not that Luke would be truly interested in her, but well, they would have pretended.

That might have been better than having her dance card filled by Dylan from Davenport.

"There won't be any relapses. I promise, I am not in love with Duncan." Anymore. "And I know he didn't love me." Even if he did. Maybe. But probably not. "And most of all, I want you to have the most wonderful day of your life." Really.

Really.

Bridgett smiled. "Thanks, sis. I know we've never been close, but the fact that you would come and help me on such short notice…" She removed a cucumber. "Maybe I overreacted by booting you off my wedding party. It was just so…unexpected. One second you were making a toast, the next, accusing me of stealing your boyfriend. As hard as it was, I had to keep the big picture in mind. My perfect day versus your pain. I really didn't have a choice. I'm sure Mom and Dad would have understood, too. They always saw the big picture." She gave her a sad smile and returned the cucumber.

The big picture. As when they'd uprooted their ten-year-old from her life in Minneapolis so their teenage daughter could pursue a life as a runway model? When her mother had moved to Milan for a year so Bridgett could get a better toehold in the modeling world, and sent Scarlett to boarding school? How about when her father used her camp tuition to fly them all over to Paris to watch Bridgett's first big show, only to leave her in the hotel room while they "networked"?

And they certainly saw the *big picture* when they'd listed Aunt Gretchen as her guardian in case of their sudden deaths. Spinster Aunt Gretchen, the hoarder who lived in a bungalow in south Rochester, hidden away behind stacks and stacks of used books.

At least after their accident, Scarlett could hide herself away, lose herself inside a different world. Every time she picked up a book, she saw herself as a new heroine, caught up in a new adventure. And yes, she loved Aunt Gretchen, despite her idiosyncrasies. She might have only known how to cook chicken potpies, but at least Aunt Gretchen never treated her like leftovers.

In fact, with Aunt Gretchen, Scarlett felt like the center of the world.

Probably how Bridgett felt every single day.

What would that be like? For someone to see only you? For all the pining she had done over Duncan, she'd seen only Bridgett in his eyes at the engagement party.

That's why Scarlett had grabbed that second glass of champagne. Everything sort of blurred after that.

"Of course I understand why you replaced me, Bridgett." What else could she say?

The technician wrapped Scarlett in a large towel then helped her ease back onto the padded table. She set two cucumber slices on Scarlett's closed eyes. "Twenty minutes. Don't move."

"Can't you just feel the minerals seeping into your pores?" Bridgett said.

She tried not to imagine tiny bugs eating away at her skin. She just wanted a shower.

"I can't wait for the party tonight. You did talk to the chef, right? About the menu?"

Talk to the chef—check.

"Would it be okay if I ditched the party, Bridge? I'm really tired." In fact, this mud only made her more exhausted, pressing into her, heating her to her bones— what was in this stuff?

"You're going to miss the party? For what, a book?" Bridgett laughed. "C'mon and live a little."

"I live just fine, thank you. I enjoy my novels."

"Your novels are wrecking your life. It's why you haven't been able to settle down, find the right job, go after the man you want. It's why you're a temp, and still single, Scarlett. You think at any moment, you're going to be caught up in some high-seas adventure, or even a spy story, and that suddenly you'll become some sort of secret agent—"

"No, I don't—"

"Oh, please. Like I didn't see the pile of suspense novels in your room."

"That was years ago. I don't have…well, I read other genres now. Like, uh, romances."

"Which is your other problem. You have in your head the perfect man, this superhero who will appear out of nowhere, march in and sweep you into his arms. I've got news for you, sweetie. He ain't comin'."

Her voice held just enough edge for Scarlet to wonder if they were still talking about her.

"No, he's just a figment of your imagination. And I promise, if he does walk in, he's got an agenda and is packing lies. So I think you need to figure out that the best guy for you is Duncan's cousin Dylan from Davenport, who may not be a superhero, but he'll come home every night and be the guy you can count on. That's reality, Scarlett, not some hunky guy out of a romance novel."

Scarlett didn't even know where to begin. Maybe she'd start with the obvious. "I don't want Dylan. And I don't need a romance hero. I just want a guy who makes me feel like…well, like I *could* be that girl in the books. Someone strong and capable and beautiful. Someone who he believes in, and who trusts him back. And it wouldn't hurt if he had strong hands."

"Fine, live in your fantasy. It's never going to happen."

Scarlett took a long breath, hating how her sister's words sank into her, found her bones.

"I can't believe I've found you. I've been looking everywhere."

The voice was very, very familiar. And welcome. Too welcome. What? How—

She reached for one of her cucumber slices, her arm crinkling against the plastic wrap as she moved.

Luke. He stood above her, looking at her as if she might be toxic.

"Hi—"

But she didn't get more than that out before he reached under her and swept her into his arms. "I need you, Scarlett," he said, and carried her from the room.

* * *

"Nice digs. What did you do to get banished to the tower, Rapunzel?" Luke stood at her window, staring down at the town of Isla Mujeres, yellow-and-red motor scooters dodging golf carts, blue boats docked at the pier, sailboats floating in the harbor.

Yes, this might be a nice place for a vacation. If he were the vacationing sort.

"Funny." Scarlett's voice came through the closed bathroom door. She'd showered at the spa to get all that mud off her while her sister had barreled out of the wrap room, her bathrobe pulled tight.

"What are you doing? Who are you?"

"I'm a friend she met on the ferry, and I need her help."

"But she's helping me!" her sister had said. She had the voice of nails on a chalkboard.

Thankfully, when Scarlett finally emerged clean and dressed, she cleared it all up before her sister unraveled. "He's a friend, sis. I promise, I'll make sure everything goes off without a hitch."

And right then, something stirred inside Luke, something he couldn't put his finger on. A calm, a loosening in his chest.

Then she turned to him and said, "How can I help?" And he decided there must have been something soothing in the mud she'd bathed in. What happened to Miss Don't-Touch-Me who he'd met in the cab?

He'd briefed her on the ride back to the hotel, and she had let him into her room, locking herself in the bathroom. Probably taking another shower. Mud, really?

But it gave him time to send her information to Artyom to create the appropriate biography, should Benito go hunting.

He turned away from the window. "I thought you had the villa."

"My sister forgot to make my reservation. I had the room that was supposed to be for her other maid of honor for one night. They forget to cancel it. But I got booted for other guests this morning. I'm probably lucky that I didn't have to sleep in one of those hammocks outside."

"Your sister forgot to make your reservation? Aren't you the maid of honor?"

"I'm a fill-in temp. I *was* the maid of honor, then I got fired and then my replacement broke her leg in Vail. So, it's back to me."

"Tough gig, being your sister's maid of honor. She's a real prize."

"You have no idea. Try being her sister." The door opened. She stood in the doorway, her skin clean, her green eyes bright even without makeup, her hair pulled back into a slick bun under a green headband. She wore a pair of white shorts, only a shade lighter than her legs, and a lime-green T-shirt. And she looked at him without a hint of chill.

In fact, he might label her look as downright warm and friendly.

Here he thought he'd get ice queen back after ousting her from her spa treatment. But she'd seemed almost, well, eager to jump on a boat teeming with terrorists for the rest of the afternoon.

Oh, why had he thought this might be a good idea?

He'd have to stick to his plan—get her on the boat then convince her to betray him. She'd get ousted, he'd get to stay. "So, how does someone get fired from being a maid of honor?"

"Easy. She accuses the bride of stealing the groom."

"Stealing the groom? As in your groom?" Ouch.

"No. Well, see, Duncan and I were good friends. We'd spent a lot of time together and I thought we were more. We held hands."

He tried not to react. Oh, he tried.

"Yes, I did read way too much into that. Obviously he wasn't into me because a measly two months after my sister breezed into town, they were an item. Six months later, well, I'm at their engagement party, champagne bubbles coming out of my nose, standing on a chair and calling her a man-stealer."

"That'll get you fired any day."

"Yep. The worst part is that even as I was saying the words, I realized the truth. He never loved me." She raised a shoulder. "I was a fool."

Yes, well he could relate to that. He almost wanted to reach over, run his hand down her arm, pull her close, because he truly understood the pain behind those words. "Considering the circumstances, I think your sister should be grateful you showed up."

She blinked at him, then smiled. "I probably owe her. And don't worry. She's not taking any chances. Remember how I thought you were my date?"

"Oh, did you? Really?"

She grinned at him. "Well, my *real* blind date showed up. Dylan from Davenport. He's a mechanic."

Luke smiled. So maybe it wouldn't exactly be torture to spend the next five hours with her. Even if they did have to end up in a nasty fight in order for her to get kicked off the boat.

More than that, he'd have to embarrass her, make her look like a tramp. A man-stealer, hopefully.

He felt a little sick. He should probably inform her of his entire plan. But his gut said she wouldn't play along, couldn't be trusted to embarrass herself. What woman would deliberately act like a floozy? Certainly not someone who looked so clean and innocent, so freshly scrubbed.

No, he couldn't tell her. Not until she couldn't back out. "I think mud becomes you," he said, then didn't know why.

"My skin feels like it's been dipped in lemon cleanser, all tingly and sharp. My sister got a yogurt wrap. I was shooting for the chocolate and coffee—oh, forget it. What's next, double-oh-seven?"

She grinned, all bright and shiny.

Uh-oh. "This isn't some sort of field trip, you know. This is the real deal. There will be men with guns. Maybe hidden, yes, but still, these aren't your neighbors in Iowa."

"Minnesota."

"Right. But the truth is, I wouldn't ask you if I didn't think I could keep you safe. I mean, they're not going to dig up the fact that you're really an undercover cop, are they?"

"What, you mean my ten years in the FBI? Not a chance. They wiped out those records when I became a receptionist." She widened her grin.

"You're real cute." He wasn't sure why he said that, but he chalked it up to that professional charm he was supposed to be using. "Here's the plan. Unfortunately, we're going to be spending the rest of the day at sea."

"Wow, that's a real bummer, especially here in the Caribbean."

He held up a finger. She closed her mouth and folded her hands. Oh, brother.

"I cannot stress enough how serious this is."

"I'm serious. I'm serious."

"Okay. Listen. You have to hang around Lucia while I try and figure out who on the boat might be trying to hurt her. Benito was right on that account—someone on the guest list wants to scare her, if not kill her, and we have to find out who. I'm going to give you a tiny alert device, and if you get into trouble or are afraid of anything—even just a shadow—you press it and I'll be there."

"Like a butler."

"Like a guy trying to keep you and Lucia from becoming shark bait. I did mention the bloody shark on the deck this morning, right?"

"On the way back to the hotel. But I was so busy picking bugs from my teeth, I wasn't sure I caught everything."

"Hey, motor scooters are the mode of transportation around here."

"I rented a golf cart. Windscreen. No bugs."

"They move at the speed of a sea slug, and I needed to find you fast."

"I'm not complaining. How *did* you find me?"

But he was stuck, for a second, on her words. *I'm not complaining.*

He hadn't complained, either, as she'd locked her arms around his waist. Something about the way she hung on as he motored through the streets, in and out of cars—

"Luke?"

"Honestly, you had me scared for a bit. I thought you'd left. I went to the cottage and the maid told me you were gone. I was already halfway to the ferry launch in my head when one of the valets I know asked if I was looking for you, and then told me he'd rented you a golf cart and given you directions to the spa."

"Raoul. He was very helpful. I need to ask him to check on the dinner menu." She made a face. "My sister is having a cookout on the beach tonight."

"I'll have you back in time, I promise."

"And how, Mr. Tour Guide, will you do that?"

"Let's get your stuff." He reached for the carry-on bag, tossed it on the bed and unzipped it.

Her smile vanished. "Whoa there, fast fingers. You're not going through my things—"

"We have to get going. I'm not sure how long they are going to be in port, and I don't want them to leave without us." He opened the suitcase. "No wonder this thing weighs a ton. I can't believe you got it in the overhead."

"Listen, a girl can't have too many books."

He reached in and pulled them out. "Six books? Six. What did you think you were going to do here? I thought you were going to a wedding."

She snatched the paperbacks from him. They flew out of her hands and onto the bed. "Yes. But, you know, just in case there was downtime."

"Downtime, or escape-from-your-sister—or should I make that blind date—time? Certainly you didn't expect to read all six of these."

"I don't know what kind of mood I'll be in. I have to bring different genres. Sometimes it's helpful for a girl to have a backup plan. Just in case Dylan from Davenport happens to be a little too handsy."

The thought churned a strange feeling inside, one he didn't want to scrutinize. He looked over at the book covers. "Looks like all the same stuff to me. What are those, bodice rippers?"

"Oh, for goodness' sake. No, most of them are romantic suspense, but this one is historical romance, and—"

"They're all romance."

"So what? I like romance."

"You know, those stories aren't real life. No one falls in love forever."

"Just like a guy doesn't come in and sweep you into his arms?" She clamped her hand over her mouth, her eyes widening.

He felt his face heating. "Well, not unless there is a national emergency." He looked back to the suitcase and started rifling through it. "Did you bring a swimsuit?"

"Yes, thank you." She grabbed at his wrist, pulled it away. "I'll pack, thanks."

"You just need a swimsuit, maybe a cover-up. And flip-flops. A hat."

She began to pile the clothes on the bed.

"I said a swimsuit."

"What do you think this is?" She held up a pair of shorts and a long tank top.

"A mumu. Where's your bikini?"

"I'm from Minnesota. I don't have a bikini. You're lucky I have these shorts."

"Okay, we'll stop by the store and get you a bikini—"

"I'm not wearing a bikini!" She picked up one of the books and threw it on the bed.

Then she glanced at him and picked it back up, turning it over to read the back.

"Do not tell me you are thinking of bringing that with you."

"Well, maybe not. I might bring a different one…"

"You're going to be spending the day on a luxury

yacht. With a very nervous bride-to-be. This is not a time to read."

"It could be. You never know when a good book might come in handy."

"Fine. Take it."

"Wait—I have to see if this is the one I want."

He grabbed the book from her and scooped up the rest of her clothing with the other hand. "Please tell me you brought a beach bag."

She held up her hands in surrender. "I just hope that's the right book." She opened the top of the suitcase and pulled out a canvas bag. "If I read the first chapter and hate it, then I'll have nothing else to read."

"Cry me a river. C'mon." He threw her stuff in the canvas bag.

"Stop." She put her hands on his chest. "Really, I need to know the plan."

"Okay…I just need you on the boat long enough to convince them that yes, you do exist and we are together. But it's not permanent. I have a plan to get you off the boat and out of this mess, so don't worry."

"Really? What kind of plan?"

By making you betray me. By pushing you into the arms of another man. By embarrassing you and throwing you off the yacht. But the words stuck inside his chest.

"Can't you just trust me?"

He didn't realize how raw and fresh those words sounded until they tumbled out, until they lay between them.

Or how much it might sting, like salt on old wounds to have her step back, smile and say, "Of course I trust you."

SEVEN

If this was the life of a secret agent, point her to the dotted line. Yes, she could get used to the attention of stewards, the ocean lapping against the hull of the boat, the laughter of guests as they motored off the end of the yacht on Jet Skis some three decks below.

Around them, as far as the eye could see, the ocean stretched out in a deep indigo, even as the sun began to bleed into the horizon.

She could also get used to Luke's almost gallant attention as he watched her through his aviator sunglasses, not to mention the feel of his hand on her back as he'd layered sunblock onto her skin. Not that SPF 30 would make her feel any less exposed than she did in the two-piece barely bikini Luke purchased for her in the gift shop. Good grief, she hadn't shown this much skin since birth. But really, it was nothing out of the ordinary here. Next to her, Lucia wore a white string top and thong. And she had the gorgeous tan that suggested she spent more time than not in her three patches of fabric and a rubber band.

Lucia lay on her back, her face to the sun, her giant bug-eye glasses covering most of her face, one arm lifted over her head as if she hadn't a care in the world.

Certainly not as if someone might be trying to kill her. Honestly, Scarlett had begun to have her doubts. But why else would Luke woo her onto this boat?

"So, you live in Minnesota?" Lucia said. Scarlett opened her eyes, realizing that their upper deck was cleared of any other souls.

"I do. I'm a receptionist. Well, last Tuesday was. Wednesday through Friday I was a file clerk at a dentist's office. And then on Friday nights, I stock books for the library, although that's just volunteer, unless a spot opens up. I really love Saturdays, though, because I've been working at this same dog kennel for three years and I just love holding the animals while Adam rinses out the stalls. Fun."

Lucia looked over at her, drew down her glasses. "You work in four different places?"

"Oh, no, I work for one company—Rochester Temps—but they send me wherever there is a need. Sometimes I temp for the same company for two or three weeks. Or I just go for a day. It depends. But at the kennel, they just keep asking me back." What would her fellow temps say if they saw her right now, getting a sleek tan on a multimillion-dollar yacht?

She'd landed the best temp gig in history.

"So, you never know where you're going to be from one day to the next?"

"Nope. It's exciting. Except, well, sometimes it can be stressful, always learning new office rules, but I've discovered that most offices have the same expectations. Come in, do your job, keep your mouth shut, adapt, smile and keep their secrets."

Luke had come off his perch by the rail to sit in a chair beside them. "Sounds a little like what I do."

It did? "Really?"

"Sure. New assignments every week, having to work with what I have."

She glanced at him, searching for indictment, but he only grinned down at her. "So, you're saying I'm sort of a secret agent?"

"Just so we're clear, my job title is security specialist, but if you want, I'll call you a secret agent." The sun on his hair turned it to bronze, and he had the nicest smile. She certainly wouldn't complain about hanging out with a guy who had the build of a hardworking man—strong arms, amazing shoulders. She had noticed, however, a webbed scar just above his knee, peeking out from below his orange swimsuit. *Sure* his job was just like hers. She didn't remember getting wounded changing the toner on a copier. Maybe someday he'd trust her enough to tell her how he got injured.

Footsteps clumped on the stairs, and Luke went to the rail. Scarlett lifted her head as Benito ascended the top step. He held a cold beer in his hand. "Roll over, *chiqua*, I don't want you to get burned."

Lucia smiled at him, greeting him with a kiss. He sat down at her feet at the end of the chaise and glanced over at Scarlett. She could admit that she'd conjured a different image in her head when Luke described him. The son of a so-called real estate mogul from Panama, she expected him to be all hairy-chested swagger. Instead, Benito seemed clean-cut, trim, even a politician of sorts, the way he greeted her when she boarded. *I'm so glad to meet my bride's best friend!*

Frankly, she had to ignore the smallest twinge of regret at her subterfuge role. She'd never been a liar. But, as Luke explained, big causes justified little lies.

Maybe.

"Hello, Benito," she said, lifting her sunglasses.

Benito ran his hand up Lucia's leg. "I went through all my guests. None of them seem to have any reason to hurt us, but I will have a man outside our door tonight." He glanced at Luke, however, as if there might be one stone unturned.

Or maybe her overactive spy brain simply imagined the sudden shift of energy when Luke turned, folding his hands over his chest.

Benito took a sip of his beer. "So, how did you two meet?" He looked at Scarlett and it took her a moment to realize that he referred not to her and Lucia, but her and Luke.

She glanced at Luke. He drew a breath.

"In Italy."

It was the first thing that came out of her mouth, and now they had to stick with it. Whoops. Luke looked at her and she smiled at him.

"Right," he said. "Uh, I was…"

"On a tour of the vineyards. I was taking a cooking class. And our tours met up for a—"

"Tasting. Only, she doesn't drink wine."

"You don't drink wine?" Benito frowned.

Scarlett picked up her now-lukewarm orange juice. "It goes right to my head. But I do like…rigatoni."

"Actually, her favorite dish is *bitecchine di cinghiale*, don't you remember, darling?" Luke grinned, something dangerous in his smile.

"Oh, yes, what did it have in it again—cheese?" She looked at him, her eyes widening under her sunglasses. He looked to be enjoying this too much.

"Wild boar and prunes. You were a pro."

She kept her smile. "But I loved what Chef Baghatti said…what was it?"

"Bellissimo?"

"No, no." She sat up, swinging her legs over the lounger. "It was such a breathtaking place. I saved for a year to be able to go, and of course, I went by myself because I was hoping I might find true love." She winked at Benito. "I was sitting in the Adirondack chair by the pool when Luke walked in, and of course, there were these two women from Paris who thought they might catch his eye. They drove me crazy the entire time, always Paris this, and Paris that—I think Chef Baghatti wanted to throw them into the wine cave and lock the door. Sure enough they got up and strutted toward Luke, and wouldn't you know it, he wasn't watching where he was going and he knocked one right into the pool."

"I didn't mean to," Luke mumbled. "I had my eyes elsewhere." His gaze tracked to her, and warmth rushed through her. She probably needed to get out of the sun.

"Anyway, Chef Baghatti saw what happened and he convinced Luke to leave his tour and join ours. Said we were aligned under the stars or something."

"Actually he said, *'Quando ì fui preso, et non me ne guardai, chè i bè vostr'occhi, donna, mi legaro.'* The words flowed out of Luke so easily, as if they really had met in Italy, really had fallen in love under a waxen moon, this exotic man and his high-adventures girlfriend. They scooped all the breath from her. Luke met her eyes with a smile that reached right through her. "When I was caught, I put up no fight, my lady, for your lovely eyes had bound me."

Oh. Uh…

"That's very romantic," Lucia said, pulling down her glasses. "So, it was love at first sight?"

"Yes," Luke said.

"Yes," Scarlett whispered.

"There is nothing sweeter than true love." Glancing at Luke, Benito nodded, camaraderie in his expression. Then he raised his bottle and Scarlett reached for her glass. She met his in a toast.

Luke's smile, however, dimmed for just a second, hidden from Benito as he picked up his sweating soda from the table. But his voice betrayed nothing amiss. "To true love."

Scarlett lay back on her lounger, his words still in her ears.

Benito finished off his beer and kissed Lucia. "I think that Scarlett and Luke should cook for us something of Tuscany."

Her mouth opened.

"Yes, Benito. We would love to, after the wedding—" Luke said, his voice easy.

"No, tonight. Cook for us tonight."

Tonight?

But Luke shrugged. "No problem. What do we need, darling?" He turned to her, took another sip of his drink.

What did they need? He didn't *seriously* believe that she'd been in Italy, right? She'd…she'd, well she'd lied. She'd never been to Italy, never even taken a cooking class. She'd simply drawn from a scene in a book—

Oh, wait. He smirked at her.

"Basil. And…" What was that other Italian herb? "Oregano. And fresh mozzarella. And—"

"I don't think we can come up with a wild boar." Benito smiled. "But I'll have my people find the rest." He kissed Lucia on the forehead. *"Salut!"*

Oh, no.

He got up and climbed down from the deck.

Luke continued to smile.

"Are you serious? We're going to cook?" Yet, for a rich, aromatic moment, she saw herself with an apron tied around her waist, Luke standing behind her, his arms encircling her, stirring tomato sauce, pressing a kiss to her neck—

"This is perfect," he said, probably reading her thoughts.

Yes, it was, wasn't it?

He set down his drink, his voice pitching low. "I couldn't figure out how to get you off the ship, but oh, Scarlett, you're brilliant."

"I am?" She was?

"Yes." He walked over and picked up her hand, kissing it.

She stared at him. "I don't understand." But she did relish the tingles that went up her arm, right into her brain.

Maybe he'd...what if he *wasn't* acting? What if he felt it, too, the sparks between them as they'd spun that lie, the taste of romance on this clear blue day. What if he really meant it?

She smiled up at him.

"You're going to get drunk and come on to Benito."

You're going to—What? "Wait! What did you say?" She yanked her hand out of his grasp. "I'm not going to do any such thing!"

His smile dimmed. "Just calm down, it's a great plan."

"It's a horrible idea. Why on earth would I ever do that? First, I don't drink—you know that."

"You don't have to drink. I'll teach you a trick that makes it look like you're drinking only you're not. You'll be sober, but Benito won't know that."

"Why would I want him to think I'm drunk?"

"Because a sober girl wouldn't try to seduce him."

"I will not try and *seduce* him! What a horrible thing to say. I'm...well, I'm a Christian for one, and two, I'm... engaged!"

And of course, her voice had to tremble, her insides suddenly jumbled. But he'd just kissed her hand, just looked at her as if he...

It was all part of the mission. Part of adapting. A temp job.

What a fool she'd been to think he might actually be interested in her. She'd blame it on her sunstroke.

She looked at Lucia. "Are you okay with this?"

Clearly not, from the stricken look on Lucia's face.

Scarlett turned to Luke. "Why?"

His smile had cooled, his expression dark. "Because, like I told you in the hotel, this is a short-term gig. You need to get off this boat. And I have to stay. And the only way I can think of is for you to offend your best friend here. Lucia, you have to kick her off, and Benito has to believe it."

Lucia sighed.

"Lucia—" Luke started.

"I know, I know. I just..." Lucia swallowed. "Fine."

"Fine?" Scarlett tore her gaze off Lucia and turned back to Luke. "No, *not* fine. This is your magnificient plan? I'm not going to have anyone think I would betray, well, my fiancé—" she pointed to Luke "—and you—" she turned to Lucia, "my best friend. What kind of person would that make me? No. I'm not a man-stealer." Her jaw tightened and she pinned a glare on Luke. "And you know it."

His mouth tightened a little around the edges. "Of course you're not. But it's a good plan, and it'll work."

"Well, what if I don't want to leave? I don't *have* to leave. Lucia needs me, right?"

"Don't answer her," Luke said darkly.

Lucia drew in a long breath.

"It doesn't matter what she says. I'm not leaving." Scarlett got up, grabbed her wrap, snaked it around her waist and slipped into her flip-flops.

"Where are you going?"

"To the kitchen. I'm going to learn how to cook."

Luke had recruited a regular Julia Child. Scarlett stood in the kitchen, a towel around her waist, slicing a piece of freshly grilled tenderloin into strips, her hair back in a curly ponytail, putting more effort into the meat than she probably needed to.

He settled his hands on her hips, intending to lean in and whisper in her ear for the benefit of Benito's chef, who now tossed an arugula salad. Scarlett jumped and rounded on him.

The knife dripped dark juice and he peddled back, hands up. "Don't kill me."

"I should." She narrowed her eyes at him, then turned back to the meat. "I still can't believe you suggested what you suggested."

He could admit that after she'd left, and he'd had a moment to allow the fresh air to clear his brain, he didn't exactly love the idea of her flirting with Benito. Something about the images of her in Benito's arms just made his stomach tighten.

"What are you making?"

"Tagliata with rosemary, capers and lemon."

"Really?"

She made a face at him. "You so underestimate me."

Yes, perhaps he did. "Can I help?"

"Sure, turn down the heat on that balsamic vinegar I'm reducing. It should be the texture of syrup." She glanced at the chef and he nodded, a smile on his face.

Luke picked up the spoon, stirring the mixture bubbling on the stove. "This smells good. And what's this?" He pushed what looked like mini artichokes around a pan seasoned with oil.

"Fried capers. I couldn't believe Estoban had them in his pantry."

"Okay, I'm impressed."

"Don't be. The recipe was in the back of one of my novels." She slid the sliced meat onto a plate layered with cut arugula. "I cooked it for my aunt, and we pretended we lived in Tuscany for the day."

"Is that where you came up with our scenario?"

"A great scene from *To Rome with Love*." She reached for a pan of oil, rosemary and garlic and drizzled it over the meat.

"Another book?"

"Same book. But one of my favorites." She picked up the caper pan, added it to the reduced balsamic vinegar and stirred. "See, life imitating art." She looked up at him, smiled, but it didn't reach her eyes.

He'd hurt her. If the bloody knife didn't give it away, the way she tucked in her arms to move past him with the pot of vinegar did.

As if she didn't want to touch him.

He suddenly very much remembered touching her, his hand rubbing sunblock over her shoulders, on her upper back, the rich smell of coconut lifting from her skin.

The fragrance caught him as she walked by, and for a second he couldn't breathe.

He watched her pour the vinegar over the steak and for a long moment, he forgot where he was. He saw himself in a kitchen, just like this, Scarlett preparing dinner, him setting the table. Perhaps she'd look up at him and smile, as she did this afternoon when they'd spun their story. He'd put down the silverware, come over to her, wrap his hands around her waist and turn her, catch her face in his hand and—

"You can put this on the table. And then fetch Benito and Lucia." She thrust the platter of meat into his hands without meeting his eyes.

Oh, boy.

He put the platter on the counter as she turned to the sink and began dumping in her used utensils. Her breaths came quickly, as if she might be trying not to cry.

He sighed.

"Scarlett, I'm sorry." He glanced at the chef, now placing salad on their plates, and stepped up to her, longing to touch her shoulder but instead leaning over to talk into her ear. "I didn't mean to hurt you. I'm just trying to keep you and Lucia safe, and I can't help but think it would be better if you got thrown off the boat."

Her breath trembled. "I know."

He stilled. "You…know?"

"Yes. And I'll do it. But I'll feel sick every second."

Yeah, well…him, too. He curled his hand over her shoulder, hating it when she stiffened. "I can't figure out how else to get you off this boat. As it is, you're going to miss your sister's party."

"Oh, she'll be distraught, I'm sure."

He didn't miss the sarcasm in her voice. "I'll have you back by morning, even if I have to hijack one of the Jet Skis."

"Terrific."

"It's just pretend, you know. You won't really be flirting with him."

She closed her eyes, her jaw tight. "Yeah. I got that part. Loud and clear."

Then why was she so upset? Certainly she knew that he didn't really think she could be a man-stealer, a betrayer? Six hours with her had told him that she was the kind of woman who would be faithful. Loyal.

Good thing they were just pretending, because she just might be the kind of woman he could trust, even... love.

What? He blew out a breath, backed away from her, gathered himself. No. He so didn't have room for a woman in his life. Not with his job taking him all over the world.

More than that, he had terrible instincts. Look what happened last time he'd given out his trust, his heart.

"I'll find Benito and Lucia," he said, more coolly than he intended.

When he returned with Benito and Lucia, he didn't recognize the woman he'd left waiting for them in the dining room. She had loosened her hair, added lipstick and held a glass of wine that he knew she wasn't drinking.

"Hey, Benito," she said in a voice that wasn't quite right. "I missed you."

Oh, brother. If this was her being seductive, they'd be shark dinner. She just might be the worst flirt on the planet.

Indeed, Benito's eyebrow raised. "You made us dinner."

"You asked me for dinner, didn't you?"

This couldn't be good. Luke pulled out her wicker chair. "Why don't we eat?"

She sat down and gave them all a sloppy smile. Really, she hadn't been drinking—had she?

Benito sat next to Lucia. And Luke wanted to cringe when Scarlett scooted her chair closer to him.

Benito took Lucia's hand. "What did you make us?"

"Tagliata. It's steak with capers and rosemary." Scarlett leaned on one hand, meeting his eyes. "I hope you like steak."

Benito picked up his knife. "It's no wild boar, but it'll do." He looked at her.

Then he made the mistake of winking.

Scarlett laughed, something high and way too bright, and Luke wanted to dive under the table.

"Oh, Benito, you are so funny!" She slammed the table and everything shook. Luke reached out, grabbing her glass before it went over.

"O-kay, I think that's enough for you." He moved the wine then slid his arm around the back of her chair while Benito eyed them. "She gets a little too friendly when she's been drinking."

"I thought she didn't drink."

"Only when I cook!" She went to bang the table again and Luke caught her hand. "How about if we leave the bride and groom to their dinner and I'll take you back to the room?"

She leaned back, put her hands over her mouth. "Oh, Lukie, I don't think that's a good idea."

Lukie?

"It's the sun, I'm sure. It dehydrates a person." He pulled out her chair, pulling her up into his arms. "Enjoy. She's a fabulous cook."

Benito rose. "Do you need help?"

"Yes, help me Benito," she said, her arm draped over Luke's neck.

Perfect. Maybe, if he'd let it play out longer, she might just get herself ousted by Benito himself. But, well, he couldn't take it. Besides, at this rate, they might both get thrown off into the sea.

He glanced at Lucia. Maybe it was enough, though, for a rousing fight in the morning, something Lucia could hurl at Scarlett. Something that might send her home. He tried to send that message to her but found her tight-lipped.

Even offended.

Okay, see, this is what he got for working with amateurs.

He pulled Scarlett from the table and let her lean against him as they walked out into the hallway.

They closed the door to the galley and in a second, she'd untangled herself from his grip and pushed him away. "What's your problem? I was doing great in there."

He grabbed her arm and pulled her down the deck, his voice low. "Are you kidding me? It was painful. Like you've never flirted with a man in your entire life. That was wretched!"

Her eyes widened and she gulped in a breath. Then, yanking her arm from his grip, she marched in front of him, nearly running.

Perfect. "Scarlett!"

"Just leave me alone, Luke. Just…I'm sorry I'm such a fool."

Oh, for crying in the sink. "You're not a fool."

She rounded and her eyes glistened against the starlight. "I am. Because, well…okay, I haven't flirted with a man. Ever. I don't know how. I just…well, apparently, my best attempts are laughable."

"That was your best attempt?"

She closed her eyes and he wanted to bang his head against something hard.

"I didn't mean it like that."

"I'm not my sister. I don't flirt. I'm just me, okay? But clearly that's not good enough. And yes, you're right. This was a mistake. I just hope…well, that I didn't destroy all your big plans."

She whirled away from him and ran up the stairs to the next deck. By the time he followed, she'd slammed the door to her stateroom.

He stood there for a long moment, then walked out onto the deck and sat down on one of the lounge chairs. He leaned back and considered the stars in the night sky.

"Having woman problems, son?"

EIGHT

The cool darkness of the stateroom—only the moonlight slanted in through the blinds—calmed the chaos in Scarlett's brain.

She shouldn't have had that sip—not even one sip!—of wine. It went straight to her head and numbed her into believing she could pull this off.

It was painful. Like you've never flirted with a man in your entire life.

Well, she hadn't, thanks. She'd hoped she could rely on her acting skills, but apparently even those turned out to be abysmal. And now, because of Luke and the way he turned her brain to oatmeal, the way he made her believe that she might be some sort of secret agent, she'd turned herself into a fool.

Again.

She slid to the floor, her back against the door, pressing her head to her knees.

No wonder she liked romance novels. Because it was all she had. After all, who would actually fall for her? The girl hidden behind the stacks of books, the temp girl, the Hanson family leftovers.

Not Duncan, of course. And clearly not Luke.

She pressed her fists into her eyes. No, she wouldn't

cry. Luke had promised her nothing. He'd made it clear from the beginning that she just had a job to do. The blame for this night's fiasco belonged to her.

And, yes, maybe she had played it up a bit. After all, a girl didn't watch her glorious sister perform all the time without learning a few tricks.

She *had* enjoyed Benito's surprise. And the way Luke grabbed for her glass, clearly distraught. Okay, so maybe she'd gone over the top, but he deserved it. Betray him? Get herself thrown off the ship? Be accused of man-stealing? Never in a thousand years.

Her smile vanished. Except at this rate, she and Luke might both be thrown off the ship and wow, had she made a mess of his mission.

She cupped her face with her hands. They reeked of garlic and rosemary. Her stomach churned. Oh, please, she just wanted to go home.

"Oh, God, I'm sorry. I'm so, so sorry." She leaned her head back against the door. "I don't know why I do this—dream up some other life for myself than the one You've given me. I have a good life—a job that I like, friends, my aunt who loves me. I don't know why I thought this might be my chance to—"

"So, you're having woman problems?"

The voice came through the door and she stilled. It sounded like Benito, only deeper. With more menace.

She got up, moving into the shadows to look out the window.

On the deck outside, Luke sat on one of the lounge chairs, his head down, his arms folded across his chest as if defeated. "Hello, Claudio. Yes. She's angry with me."

A bigger man leaned on the rail, not far from him. Claudio? Benito's father?

She stepped closer to the window, held her breath.

"I've been watching you two."

Luke's head came up.

"It's my job. People are always trying to worm their way into my family, and I have to watch out for snakes." Claudio took a drink of whatever he held in his hand. "There's something off with you two. I know you said you were engaged, but she doesn't look like a woman in love. She looks like a woman trying to make you happy. A woman you might have hired."

Did he just call her a prostitute?

"Are you calling my fiancée a…hooker?" His voice held indignation.

Thank you, Luke.

"I'm just saying that I don't think she's quite what you think. Or maybe *you're* not quite what we think."

Uh-oh…

Luke gave a weak laugh, and hello, if he thought her flirting sounded pitiful—

She opened the door, stepped out onto the deck. "Luke, honey, are you coming in?" And she even added a tremble, as if she might be worried.

Luke looked at her, swept the surprise from his face, smiled. "In a minute."

But a minute might be too late, gauging by the expression on Claudio's face—the narrowed eyes, the way he considered her. She closed the door and walked out onto the deck into the moonlight. "No. Now. I'm so sorry I got angry with you. I just want to make sure I get some shopping in, but I know how you hate it. How about if I go to the mainland tomorrow? You can stay here."

She turned to Claudio. "That would be okay, right?"

"Of course. We'll be docking in the morning to check

on the preparations for the rehearsal dinner and the wedding."

"Perfect." She kept her smile and sat down next to Luke on the chaise. Lifting her hand, she ran it down his face, catching his eyes. "I want to make my future groom happy."

And, despite the melodrama of the words, she delivered them from a place inside that didn't seem pretend. They felt, in fact, much too real. They shook through her, made her catch her breath, look away.

She caught Claudio with his eyes on her, as if testing her words.

What was a girl to do? She turned back to Luke, leaned forward and kissed him.

She'd expected something halfhearted from him, something to remind her that he was only pretending, but he must be a better actor than she gave him credit for because his hand came up, caught in her loose hair, and he pulled her against him.

She knew she shouldn't enjoy it, shouldn't let the feel of his lips on hers go to her head, but...

But his other arm came around her and tucked her into the pocket of his arms. Then, he kissed her back. His kiss swept every thought from her head—the romance of the sea, the gentle rock of the boat, the sound of the night. All of it lost as she let herself sink into his arms.

Luke.

His hands tangled in her hair, and when she pulled away, he met her eyes. For a flash, she glimpsed something unmasked in them.

Fear, maybe. A vulnerability.

Then he blinked and the game resumed in his smile. "Yeah, baby, it's time for bed." He took her hand, pulling them both to their feet. *"Buenos noches,"* he said to Claudio, then led them to the cabin.

He wasn't really going to sleep in her stateroom, was he? But of course, they were supposed to be engaged. Assumptions had clearly been made. Thankfully the room had an inner bedroom off the living room.

She entered behind him and watched him shut the door.

She could still feel herself in his arms. Oh, wow, this would hurt tomorrow when she walked away from him. When she took Dylan's arm at Bridgett's wedding and pretended to want to be there.

"I'm sorry I let you down tonight, Luke."

He glanced up at her, his eyes unreadable. He had such beautiful eyes—she hadn't really noticed them before, how golden brown they were, how they could pull her heart from her chest.

"You were…brilliant." His voice emerged rough, as if rife with some sort of emotion.

"What?"

"You were brilliant out there with Claudio. I…wow. I'm the one who's sorry. You're right. I underestimated you."

"It's the least I could do. And now you're off the hook. Tomorrow I'll leave, and you can stay. Good luck."

She turned to go, but he caught her arm.

And in that moment, with the moonlight puddling on his face, with his eyes shining, she just wanted to step into his arms and kiss him all over again.

But this was pretend. Period.

As if to remind her, Luke said softly, "Thanks for being a such a good sport."

Right. A good sport in their *game*. She nodded, pulling herself away. "Not one foot off the sofa, bub, or you'll regret it."

He smiled at her joke and she tried to match it. But it probably came out foolish, just like her. So, she fled to the bedroom, locked the door and pressed a pillow to her face lest he hear her cry.

The nightmare always started with a knock on the door. Regardless of where he found himself standing in the dream—at the picture window overlooking the D.C. cityscape, or in the bathroom, staring at his bloodshot eyes, or even sitting on the side of the bed, watching Darcy sleep—the knock startled him, brought him to his feet, to the door.

And every time, although he expected it, although he'd lived through it, he opened the door unguarded, as if expecting a tray of breakfast. Instead—and too often he woke himself up with a roar of warning—a man the size of a linebacker stood in the hallway, his eyes dark, his fist already cocked. Luke jerked, even in his sleep, as the blow landed on his jaw, as he spilled back into the room.

Sometimes, pain even exploded through his head, down his spine, shaking through him as he turned, fell to his knees.

Tried to clear his head.

"Gary, what are you doing here?" Darcy said as she roused, her eyes on his assailant. Something cold slicked through him.

She knew the man.

Worse, as she clutched the sheet to herself, as her eyes rounded, the truth hit Luke in the solar plexus.

She was married.

And when Gary grabbed him again by the collar, he

didn't even throw his hands up to protect himself. He just took the blow because he deserved it.

Still, he should have stood in the way when Gary grabbed his wife, when he shoved her toward the door, scooping up her clothing. And when Darcy turned back, fear in her eyes, he should have run after her.

Only this time, when she turned in the dream, it wasn't Darcy who peered back at him, who mouthed his name, whose hazel-green eyes spilled over with tears.

Scarlett.

And Gary—he had changed, too. No longer the irate former D.C. cop, estranged from his wife but still very possessive of her, his face morphed, darkened, twisted—

Benito.

Luke stood, shaken, pain seeping into his body, glued to the floor as Benito jerked Scarlett's arm, as he yanked her out into the hotel hallway.

No—no— "No! Stop!" Why couldn't he move? His body had gone dead, paralyzed. "No!"

"Luke, wake up. Luke!"

He felt hands on him, and the voice reached into the nightmare to pull him free, to propel him out of the icy grip of fear and into—

Their darkened stateroom. Kneeling next to the sofa, her cool hand on his shoulder, Scarlett peered down at him, concern on her face.

"You were yelling. At high decibels. I had to stop you before the coast guard banged down the door. Who's Gary? And who can't he have?"

Luke sat up, the sheet falling to his waist. The air-conditioning raised gooseflesh on his skin. He shivered and reached for his shirt, draped over the back of the sofa. Scarlett got up and stepped back, her arms folded over herself as he pulled it on.

His hands shook as he fumbled with the buttons.

"Luke?"

He left the buttons and put his feet on the floor, needing something to steady himself. "I don't want to talk about it."

She didn't move. He waited for her to leave but she simply stood there.

"What?"

"Please. Really? I'm going to go back to sleep after that?" Her voice softened, and then she sat down on the arm of the sofa. "You know, strangers make good listeners."

Only she wasn't a stranger, was she? Not after they'd spent the day together. Not after—

The kiss. That's what triggered the dream. The kiss that she'd delivered after cluing into Claudio's curiosity. The kiss that had probably saved his hide—both their hides. The kiss that had turned into something dangerous, because suddenly he'd forgotten why he was on the yacht, forgotten Lucia and the Sanchez family, and only Scarlett remained—her soft lips, the way she curved into his arms. She smelled good, too—coconut oil, the salt of the sea. Yes, he'd forgotten his mission and simply wanted to disappear with her, in that moment when he'd felt safe.

Trusted.

He wanted to be with a woman he could trust, who trusted him back. Someone with whom he didn't fear betrayal.

Someone, perhaps, like Scarlett.

They were in big trouble. Because small mistakes led to gigantic ones, the kind where people ended up hurt. Or dead. "I apologize, Scarlett. I never should have kissed you."

He expected something of a flinch, perhaps, but she seemed nonplussed, lifting her shoulder. "I know it's all a part of the cover. An act. Nothing but pretend."

Her words stung more than they should have. Because with her sitting there, the moonlight turning her eyes to emeralds, he didn't want it to be pretend.

A lifetime ago, he might not have cared. He might have taken that line between pretend and reality and wiped it right out.

But today, he cared. Today he wanted to be the kind of man who didn't have to apologize to himself, to God.

Maybe she saw it in his eyes, too, because she came over and sat beside him. "What is it?"

He couldn't look at her. Not without wanting to kiss her again.

"I just have to make sure we stay focused." He ran his hands through his hair.

"Of course we will." But her voice wavered, just a bit. As if she didn't believe her own words.

He knew she didn't understand. They *had* to keep this pretend. "Listen to me. That wasn't just a nightmare—it was a memory." Maybe if he told her the kind of man he truly was... "I got someone I cared about killed."

He didn't want to look at her but he couldn't help it. Perhaps he longed for the disgust, something to really shake reality into her. But no—concern, even sorrow, creased her face.

"Oh, Luke, I'm so sorry."

He got up, put space between them.

"But you were calling my name, too."

He was? He looked at her.

"What happened, Luke?"

He turned away from her. She looked so sweet and pretty in the moonlight. "I was in a dark place. I had just left the military—or rather, the military had left me. I had a lot of anger." He stood at the window. "My father was a jerk and he left me and my mom when I was thirteen. He already had another family in a different city. But the affair that broke my mother happened in our own home."

He could still hear the shouting if he let himself. "She found him in their bed with the neighbor. One of her best friends."

"I'm sorry."

He shoved his hands into his pockets, turned and looked at her. "I hate adultery. I caught one of my superior officers stepping out on his wife during an overseas R and R and it just pushed all my buttons. I sort of lost it. It was the last of too many fights, and it wasn't beyond me that maybe I'd worked out my anger at my father on the guys who I saw betraying their wives. But the navy doesn't appreciate baggage, and they didn't ask me to reenlist. In fact, they discharged me without honors."

"Oh, Luke."

"Yeah, well, guess what?" He looked away from her. "Like father, like son."

Again, nothing. She just stared at him. This woman was not *at all* what he expected.

"I came back to D.C., bunked with my mother and promptly made a mess of my life. Drinking and fighting, and I met this girl at a bar and we hooked up almost right away. Had a weekend romance that I declared true love. I was ready to propose when I answered a knock on the hotel room door. In comes her husband, leading with a right hook, and I went down hard. Not just from his cheap shot, but because I realized, right then, I'd turned into my dad. Of course, she was married."

"You weren't being your dad, Luke."

He looked at her then, wanting to believe the grace in her eyes.

"I was on my way, for sure. I couldn't believe she'd lied to me, so I did nothing when her husband dragged her out of the room, and nothing when she looked at me, terror in her eyes. I should have known, but my pride—and probably my shame—wouldn't let me move. I couldn't believe she'd betrayed me." He blew out a breath. "Or that I'd betrayed myself."

"What happened?"

"The next morning, her body showed up in the alley outside the hotel."

"Luke—" She started for him, but he couldn't take that.

He held out a hand. "Don't. The only thing good that came out of it was finding myself at her funeral, lurking in the back, hoping no one saw me. There, God got my attention. I ended up at the altar, long after they'd taken the casket away. The pastor found me, and God did, too. I walked away from the old Luke, became a new Luke. A guy who works hard to keep his promises. To not betray anyone."

"To keep people safe."

She crossed the room and stood in front of him. Oh, he wanted to touch her, to press his hand to her face. "Yes."

"But it still haunts you. The memory of letting her go."

He found himself caught in her gaze. Somehow he nodded.

"You need to forgive yourself, Luke."

"I've tried. But I can't get past the fact that although I know God has forgiven me, I can't erase what happened. Sure, I'm sorry, but that doesn't change what I did. And therefore, I can't imagine why God would be on my side. I keep waiting for Him to betray me, to walk away."

She took his hand but he couldn't look at her.

"God isn't like your father, Luke. He's not going to betray you. And he doesn't treat us as we think we should be treated."

She said the words so softly, they shouldn't have hurt the way they did. And he didn't need to flinch. But he did.

She reached up and pressed her hand to his face. Soft against rough, cool against the heat of the sun.

"I know. But I just can't get it from my head to my heart."

"You're not like your father, either, Luke."

"I'm trying not to be. I keep thinking, what if it's in the genes? What if I was born with an adulterer's heart?" What if he never figured out what had made his father roam, so he could turn it off in himself? "I haven't exactly dated since."

Something flashed in her eyes but she blinked and it was gone. "Not everyone is like that woman who lied to you."

He heard her, then. Heard the words she meant. *I'm not like the woman who lied to you.*

Or perhaps he only hoped he'd heard it. Because the words swept over him like a cool, sweet rain, into his bones, his heart.

Scarlett.

He pressed his hand to hers. He wanted to kiss her. To pull her close, hide her in his embrace, kiss her with the emotions that buzzed right under his skin. Something about her—the way she looked at him, maybe, so much trust in her eyes.

Or acceptance. Yes. His story, his sins, hadn't rattled her, hadn't sent her running. And perhaps that, more than anything, was what stopped him.

He could love her. The thought coursed through him. He could love her—her creativity, her courage, the way she kept up with him—and in a second he saw himself with her. He saw a future together.

Oh, wow. He pushed her hand away, breaking from her before he did something stupid. Pretend. This was only *pretend.*

Well, maybe not this part, the part where he found himself alone with her in the stateroom, thoughts of her in his arms cascading through his brain. No, this was very painfully real.

And this part could get them both killed. Because what she didn't get was that, standing at the doorway, seeing the fear in Darcy's eyes, his soldier instincts should have kicked in. He should have thought further than his hurt to ask why she'd stepped out on her husband. Why his name on her lips resounded with fear. Why she looked back at Luke with terror, not shame.

Instead, he'd focused only on her betrayal, and it blinded him to the danger wrestling her away.

Yes, pretend could swiftly turn to reality if Scarlett kept looking at him like that. He wouldn't see what was coming, could let Lucia—and even Scarlett herself—walk right into danger.

So he marched over to the sofa, grabbed the sheet and a sofa pillow, tucked them under his arm and headed toward the door.

"Where are you going?" Scarlett didn't exactly stand in front of the door, but she didn't move, either.

"Outside. I need fresh air. Lock the door behind me."

She moved aside. He didn't dare look at the hurt on her face.

NINE

"Where on earth have you been? I've been worried sick about you."

Bridgett glanced over at Scarlett as she stepped out onto the balcony off her sister's villa.

Oh, sure she had. In fact, Bridgett appeared downright wrung out with concern, wrapped in a fluffy cotton bathrobe, lounging on a chaise under an oversize umbrella on the deck outside her villa, her hair wrapped in a turban, zinc oxide slathered on her nose and lips. Someone, please, get a doctor.

"You don't have to get snippy about it. I really was worried."

Oops, had Scarlett said that out loud? She sank down into the opposite chaise and drew in a breath of the ocean, crashing and frothing on the coral and rocks below. The sky appeared nearly cloudless, save for the rim of darkness on the far horizon. "I'm sorry, I just meant—"

"I mean, one minute you're getting a body wrap, the next some strange man practically carries you off. Did I mention that he told me he'd have you back by dinner?"

He did? So perhaps that accounted for Luke's quietness this morning, the way he stood at the rail, watching the boat skim the waves toward shore. He'd seemed friendly enough on the surface, but anyone who really knew him could tell that something ate at him.

Except she didn't really know him, did she? Scarlett thought she'd had a glimpse, for a second, last night. The man behind the façade, the man awakened by his own failures.

I couldn't believe she betrayed me...or that I'd betrayed myself.

She saw it all as he'd explained it—the horror on his face as he realized that his girlfriend had duped him, that he'd aided and abetted her cheating on her husband.

Never mind that he'd slept with a woman he wasn't married to. But he'd explained that part, too, and she saw his desire to be a new Luke, a man who worked hard to keep his promises.

Not everyone is like that woman who lied to you.

She hadn't quite meant to put so much vulnerability into her voice when she said that, but it slipped out anyway, and for a second, when he'd looked up at her, all the pretend vanished.

At least for her it had.

For a long—too long—moment, she wished herself into his arms, kissing him without the performance and instead with what had started to stir in her heart.

No, for her, it had ceased to be pretend. So she'd had to...well, pretend.

She'd had to act as if it hadn't nearly turned her inside out to see him crying out in his sleep, to see the torment in his eyes at his own guilt, his own shame. She had to act as if she didn't want to take him into her arms and soothe away the demons.

Today, when she'd left him on the boat, she had wanted with everything inside to hole up in her cabin and refuse to leave. She'd even managed to let him kiss her goodbye—a peck really, one that had the warmth of the Minnesota she'd left behind—without clinging to him.

Because, for Luke, it was all still pretend.

And not only that, but now she knew why. He'd never let himself love someone he couldn't trust. Someone he thought might betray him.

Not everyone is like that woman who lied to you.

And the life he'd chosen certainly didn't give him any chances to change that, did it? Good grief, he not only expected her to betray him, he'd practically demanded it.

Bridgett was still rattling on about her disappearance and how she'd missed the barbecue and—

"And of course, I don't mind so much if you want to explore the island, but you have a perfectly good date, you know. Dylan waited for you at the party, but you didn't show up. He's a nice guy, and you'd like him."

"I don't need help finding men."

And as soon as the words left her mouth, Scarlett wanted to grab them back.

"Oh, really? Because who is that guy, Scarlett? He looks like trouble to me. You know, I've been around the world quite a bit, and met all sorts of men, and he has a definite rogue aura about him. I'll bet he's a player."

"Like a gambler?" Because, yes, Luke definitely played a dangerous game.

"No. A playboy. A man who uses women." Bridgett pointed at her, her green eyes hidden behind her sunglasses. "Take it from me, you need to stay away from those types."

She put so much vehemence into her voice, Scarlett believed her. She had no doubt her sister had met exactly that kind of man before she wound up in Rochester, Minnesota.

Why she'd ended up in Rochester, Minnesota, Scarlett never really knew. Bridgett did an effective job of dodging that question with, "I needed a change."

Apparently that change meant invading Scarlett's ordered life, turning it upside down.

But she couldn't begrudge her sister a happy-ever-after, even with Duncan.

Duncan. Funny, she hadn't thought about him in, oh, over twenty-four hours. That felt good.

"Luke's not a player."

"Then what's he doing with you?"

Ouch. "Why, thank you, Bridgett. Because what man would want to be with me if he wasn't using me?"

Then again…

She blinked back a sudden burning in her eyes.

Bridgett reached for a glass of sweating orange juice. "Now you're just putting words in my mouth. You know what I mean."

No, she didn't. But she probably didn't want to, either.

"He's a friend, nothing more. But if it will make you feel better, I'll be sure to lift his wallet and you and Duncan can run it for prints."

"You laugh, but this is how innocent, unsuspecting women get burned."

She wasn't an—well, yes, innocent, but certainly not unsuspecting, was she? Oh, she could taste the words on her lips—*I spent the day on a yacht, protecting a mole in the Sanchez family*. But even as she rolled them around her mouth, they had the feel of the fantastical.

She probably wouldn't even believe herself if she said it out loud.

"I'm sorry I wasn't here for the barbecue, Bridge. I'll be around from here on out."

And she would, because Luke had made a point of asking her if she felt better, and suggesting that perhaps she should spend the next twenty-four hours on land after she got done shopping.

Clearly her vicious bout of seasickness had returned.

Lucia was due to get married tomorrow evening anyway, and by that time, the notorious Augusto Sanchez should have arrived, just in time for the CIA or whoever to move in. With great relief, Scarlett had done the math and realized that Bridgett, getting married on the far side of the resort, would already be down the aisle and on her way to her reception, safely out on the dinner yacht when the fireworks started.

"Yeah, I'm sorry you weren't here, too, because you were supposed to approve the menu—"

"I did approve the menu." She had, hadn't she? Or had she been too busy being swept up into Luke's world of high-stakes suspense?

"If you were, then how did I end up like *this?*" She opened her bathrobe. An angry rash layered her skin—a mesh of reddened bumps that started from her collarbone and disappeared down the V of her swimsuit.

"What is it?" Scarlett reached out as if to touch it, then yanked her hand back.

"An allergic reaction! And recoil is exactly what Duncan is going to do on our wedding night, I just know it."

Duncan had let Scarlett into the room earlier, barely

acknowledging her as he'd brushed by her. Trouble in paradise?

"How did it happen?"

"Mushrooms! They used a mushroom bullion in the marinade for the shish kebabs. Twelve hours ago, I couldn't even feel my lips and my eyes swelled shut. It was a good thing one of my bridesmaids had some allergy tablets, or I'd be in the hospital. As it is, I have to keep taking oatmeal baths." She lowered her dark glasses, and yes, she still appeared puffy around the eyes. She pressed on a couple of the hives. "I think they're going down…" She glanced at Scarlett, with what looked like hope. "They'll go down, right?"

"By tomorrow morning?" Scarlett opened her mouth, searching for the right words.

"No, we have to move the wedding to tomorrow night. I can't walk down the aisle pimply and ugly." Bridgett's voice wavered, and if Scarlett didn't know her better, she might have thought her sister would burst into tears. But Bridgett didn't cry. She simply ordered.

"You have to rearrange everything, Scarlett. Talk to the caterer, the yacht driver, the wedding guests. You have to fix this."

Scarlett stared at her. Fix this? Somewhere in the back of her mind something niggled, a sort of moan, or perhaps screaming, but she couldn't grasp it. "I don't know…"

From across the ocean, probably from the port, a horn sounded.

Then, with a whoosh, realization hit her hard. "No, no, you can't change the wedding. That won't work, not at all." Because she had no doubt that Augusto Sanchez would not go quietly into the night, or into the custody of the authorities, which meant that innocent bystanders, like her sister, might get caught in the cross fire.

Bridgett frowned at her. "What are you talking about? Of course I have to change the wedding! I can't walk down the aisle looking like I have the measles."

Scarlett schooled her voice, forcing the panic away. "You're beautiful, sis, I promise. Duncan won't even notice on your wedding day. He'll be focused on you."

"He won't notice? What, do you think he's blind?"

Her mouth opened.

"Oh, wait, of course you do. Because he didn't see how much you loved him—how much you *still* love him. Of course you want me to walk down the aisle a mess. Because you're trying to sabotage my happy day!"

"Bridge—" Scarlett could hear warning sirens.

"I'm not going to let you wreck my wedding." Bridgett pulled off her towel and shook out her long blond hair. "I knew that's why you really came. You didn't want to help me—you wanted to try and persuade Duncan not to marry me."

"Why would I—"

"You probably told the chef to put in the mushroom bouillon—"

"Don't talk crazy—"

"And that's why you weren't there! I should have guessed it!" Bridgett stood over her now, shaking.

Scarlett took a breath and backed away. "I didn't do anything of the sort, Bridgett! Get ahold of yourself!"

"Then why don't you want me to have my wedding tomorrow night?" She slapped her hands on her hips, glaring at Scarlett.

And Scarlett had nothing. Well, nothing but the truth, but that just might be worse than nothing.

"Perfect. The one person I thought I could count on.

I should have known better. You've been sabotaging me my entire life."

"What?" Hey, now, Scarlett wasn't the one who dragged the family around the world, parted her sister from friends, forced her to retreat into a world of books. "You're the one who sabotaged lives. You and your precious modeling career."

"My modeling career fed you and paid for your college education. You don't seriously think that Aunt Gretchen had enough money to feed and clothe you, did you? I sent her checks every month. Which I would have never had to do if Mom and Dad hadn't been killed trying to get back for one of your stupid theater performances."

Everything inside Scarlett stilled, her thoughts simply wiped clean, her body without feeling. Her voice came out wire-thin. "What are you talking about?"

"Oh, don't play stupid. Dad—it was always Dad— said they had to get back home because you were in some silly play."

A silly play. *Twelfth Night.* "I was Olivia."

"Whatever. I was doing a photo shoot for *Vogue*. *Vogue*. I'm not sure if you've heard of it. And they left to go see your little high school play."

"I'm sorry." She wasn't sure why she said it, perhaps simply because that's what she'd said that night when the prep school director came into the theater, took her aside, told her the news.

I'm sorry.

"Whatever. Everything has to revolve around you, Scarlett. I'm not sure why—maybe it's because you don't feel important. But you always have to be the heroine and save the day. Oh, I'm an idiot—of course! You keep your silly temp jobs because you *like* being the savior!

The one in the red cape. Well, you can put away your cape, honey, because I don't need anyone to save me, or this wedding. In fact, I should have stuck to my gut instincts. You. Are. Fired. Get out of my villa. I'm getting married tomorrow night and you'd better be far, far away."

"Bridgett."

But she'd turned away, her hand snaking up her sleeve to scratch.

"You did what?" Even ten thousand miles away, across two oceans and seven time zones, Luke had to hold the phone from his ear.

"What do you mean you recruited a civilian? Unarmed, untrained, unprotected—"

"I protected her, Chet." Well, as well as a guy could while trying to sleep outside on the deck, his eyes glued to both Lucia's and Scarlett's stateroom doors the remainder of the night.

Not that he'd gotten any shut-eye anyway. The minute he let himself doze off Scarlett and those gorgeous doe eyes came back into his brain and turned it to knots.

Or he had nightmares of Claudio figuring out how he'd been played, grabbing Scarlett and making everyone pay.

So, yeah, maybe he'd put the phone back to his ear and let Chet have at it. "I admit that it might have been a bad idea."

"Bad? Try catastrophic. What were you thinking?"

Maybe he hadn't been. Maybe Luke had simply panicked. But it seemed like the right thing at the time—all the way up to that kiss.

In fact, she played the part so well, it felt as if he

might actually have been kissing his real fiancé goodbye today, when he'd spun the story of her being seasick.

One that she reacted to appropriately by holding her stomach and nearly racing off the yacht.

He watched her go and felt a little sick himself.

Now he got up, leaned against the open door of his villa and stared at the blue sky, trying not to think of Scarlett.

"I was thinking that Lucia was scared to death, and that if I wasn't on board, she might just ditch the entire shindig, not to mention there might really be someone out to hurt her. We found a speared shark outside her door yesterday morning."

"A shark?"

"Yeah—as in, the Sanchezes have a way of making people shark bait."

"So who do you think it could be?"

"I don't know. I spent the day watching everyone on the boat—no one seemed overly interested in the bride. Except Benito, of course."

"Do you think it's him?"

"I hope not. This entire mission seems to be one snafu after another."

"Okay, okay, calm down. I was wondering what happened—I got a text from Stacey that her plane was delayed."

"She never showed, and Scarlett got in my cab instead. She seemed—well, I know she's not an agent, Chet, but she's fast on her feet. She duped Claudio not once but twice, and even made a gourmet Italian dinner for Benito and Lucia."

"Stop. Just…stop."

Luke heard a sigh on the other end of the line. "What?"

"I just want you to be careful. I hear it in your voice—it's more than admiration. You care about this woman."

"Of course I care about her. She's been a real trooper—"

"No, I mean *care*. Like you cared about Darcy." Chet had just started recruiting him around then, and he and Chet had a number of long phone conversations, during which Luke realized he could happily work for—and be friends with—ex-Delta Force captain Chet Stryker. Probably he'd let him too far into his personal life, however. But he'd had to give the man a reason why he'd wanted to get out of D.C. and start his new job, ASAP.

"Scarlett is nothing like Darcy. Nothing."

Chet didn't respond and Luke walked out to the villa porch, watching the surf froth in the coral baths below.

"You have to get rid of her, Luke. I don't care how. She's not safe."

"She's my fiancée."

"Try not to say that with so much conviction."

"I'm just pointing out that the Sanchezes might not buy the whole seasick thing for the wedding." He was hoping so, but Benito had already asked about her, twice.

"Then figure out how to break up."

Luke ran a hand down his face. "Tried that. I wanted her to betray me, maybe come on to Benito. She…she's not great at betrayal. But if I break up with her, then I get booted from the party and she stays. Then Lucia has no one. I needed Lucia to feel betrayed and kick Scarlett off the boat, but she didn't quite catch on. Now, they're actually bonding and I think Lucia feels safer with her than she does with me."

Chet said nothing while the breakers roared below. Finally, "Just keep them both safe, and try not to get yourself killed in the process. I'll see you in twenty-four."

"What? Wait, you're coming here?"

"I'm packing my sun block now. I'll be in touch." The line clicked off and Luke closed his phone. In his head, he'd hatched a loose plan last night to claim sickness. With luck, he'd get Lucia to "check in" on her friend right before the ceremony…and in time to whisk Lucia away before the fireworks. Of course, Scarlett, hopefully, would be long gone.

Long. Gone.

He tried not to let those words choke the air out of him.

Lord, I'm so sorry I got Scarlett into this mess. Please help me keep her safe.

"You. Are. Fired. Get out of my villa!"

The voice carried over the top of the waves, and it sounded so familiar.

There, below him, next door, a woman—yes, Scarlett's sister—leaned against the rail, wrapped in a bathrobe.

And there was Scarlett now, touching her sister's arm. Even Luke winced as her sister shrugged her away. "I don't care if I ever see you again."

Scarlett stood there for a long moment, as if waiting for a response. Then Luke saw her withdraw.

The sister never moved.

What was that about?

Before he could stop himself, he turned away from

the surf, walked through the villa, and opened his door just as Scarlett passed by outside.

He could have stayed silent, let her walk by, out of his life, out of his reach.

Could have retreated back to his quiet, protected world.

But the gentle touch of her hand last night as she'd pulled him out of his nightmare lingered, and he called out, "Scarlett!"

She turned. And his heart nearly left his chest when he saw her wipe her cheek.

She'd been crying.

He shouldn't descend his stairs, shouldn't catch up to her, shouldn't put his arms around her, as if they might be a real couple. But he had apparently stopped listening to himself and had started to act on instinct.

And this instinct, for the first time in years, felt right. "Are you okay?"

She pushed on his chest a little, disentangling herself from his arms. "I'm sorry."

"What happened? I heard your sister yelling."

"She fired me from her wedding."

"Again?" He didn't mean to say it quite that way. "I'm sorry."

But despite the crushed look on her face, a smile started to sneak onto her lips. She pressed a hand to her beautiful mouth and it seemed she couldn't decide between crying or laughing. "Yes…I can't seem to keep the job." Her attempt at humor dissolved, however. "My sister ate mushrooms."

Her sister ate mushrooms? "I don't understand."

"She's allergic to mushrooms, and I forgot to ask the chef to make sure there were no mushrooms in the food last night. Apparently they put mushroom bullion into the marinade and now she's covered in hives and she wants to move the wedding to Saturday night."

"Saturday night? The same time of the Sanchez wedding? That's a terrible idea. We can't risk any collateral damage. You can't let her do that."

"In case you missed something, I was fired. From being the maid of honor. I think her words were something like, 'Stay away from my wedding.'"

"Why did she fire you? I mean, it was just a mistake."

She pressed her fingers to her temples as if trying to clear her head. "She thinks I'm still after her fiancé."

"No."

"Yes."

He walked with her down the coral path. Something about her demeanor...the way she kept sighing, shaking her head, suggested there might be more. "Scarlett, what aren't you telling me?"

She stopped. Looked away, past him and into the surf. Shook her head again.

"I am your fiancé, you know. You can tell me anything."

That earned him the smallest of smiles. But it vanished as her hand brushed her shiny cheek. "I can hardly believe she said this, but she said it was my fault that our parents died. That they were headed home from New York City to my play. Of course, I had hoped they'd come—I was in a boarding school in Minneapolis." She moved forward to the beach, kicking through the sand. Her voice seemed to recover. "I can't figure her out. My entire life, from the age of ten, was about following her around the world, supporting her career. My parents finally put me in boarding school when I was fourteen to give my life some stability." She waded into the water, the waves washing upon her feet. He joined her, letting his toes sink into the sand. "They died when I was sixteen."

"I'm so sorry about your parents."

She glanced at him, her eyes shining in the night. "It was a long time ago. But their deaths left a pretty big hole in my life." She reached down, picking up a starfish as if it might be glass. "I've always been amazed by these. Did you know they can lose one of their arms and it will grow back?"

He watched her face as she lifted it to the sun, something sweetly honest about the way she stared at the starfish.

"This is my first time at the ocean. I always wanted to see it, but we never had time." The wind took her hair, wound it around her face. He barely stopped himself from pulling it away, wrapping the strands around his fingers. "We were going to go when I was twelve, during winter break from school, but that's the year my sister got her first big international gig and my mother had to take her to a photo shoot that week for some magazine."

"Sounds like your life revolved around your sister's career."

"She got her big break when she was fourteen. It only seemed right that we support her."

"And you?"

"My father stayed home with me while my mother traveled with Bridgett at first. And then we started to travel with her, and they homeschooled us. Then, finally, my parents moved to Italy with my sister and they sent me to boarding school in Minnesota."

"I'm sorry."

"Don't be. I loved it. I got involved in theater and

wrote for the campus newspaper. And then…then they were killed and the funds dried up and I moved in with my aunt."

"And your sister?"

"She went on to become a supermodel in Europe."

"And now she's marrying Duncan? Don't take this the wrong way, but…"

"Something doesn't compute? I know. But she won't tell me why she just appeared one day in Rochester. She seems to be set on marrying him and settling down as a desperate housewife, so who am I to argue? We haven't been close for ages. The last happy moment I remember was the Christmas before she started modeling." She dug her toe into the sand.

"We put on a song and dance—you know the sisters' song from *White Christmas?*"

Maybe. He might have seen it once. "Nothing comes between my sister and me?"

"That's the one. We did it for our parents on Christmas Eve. It was the last time we ever shared the limelight. But see, I adored her, I wanted her to succeed. I was enthralled with her life." She traced the starfish. "In fact, when I was sixteen I even auditioned. I didn't tell anyone who I was, but I figured, if my sister was gorgeous, certainly the agents would see something in me. So I dressed up and went in for an interview with an agency that was recruiting and…" Her shoulder lifted, then fell.

And?

He waited for it as she searched for the words. His chest tightened the longer it took.

"They told me that I didn't have a future in modeling." Her tone said their words hadn't been quite that polite. She sighed. "I realized then that I was supposed to stay in the shadows."

He didn't agree with that at all, but she probably wouldn't hear his words of protest. Not right now, at least. "What happened with you and your aunt?"

"She still lives in Rochester. I visit her on Sunday afternoons, for chicken potpies and book reviews. Romances, don't ya know." She looked up and winked at him.

That wink could make him forget his name.

She turned back to the sea, put the starfish down in the waves and lifted her face to the sun. "'Let my heart, the sea of restless waves, find peace in you, O God.'" She glanced at him. "Augustine wrote that. My heart, the sea of restless waves." She drew in a breath. "My sister accused me of always wanting to be the center of attention."

"Oh, that's rich, coming from her." He'd met her sister, thank you.

"She might be right. She said that's why I never keep a job—because I always want to be the savior." She lifted a shoulder. "I do like showing up to save the day. Maybe I've always had a bit of heroine wannabe inside of me."

"I think you have a lot of heroine inside of you," he said softly.

She smiled, the cutest dimple forming on her cheek. "That's sweet of you, but you and I both know I am not a heroine. I'm just a temp. And really, I don't have to be the center of attention. At least, I don't have to be special to the world. I'd be happy to just be special to one person."

You're special to me. The words filled his mouth and he wanted to let them free. Dip his hand into hers, pull her close and forget that they were supposed to be pretending.

Because this moment didn't feel like pretend. No, as she looked up at him and met his eyes, it felt real.

"I'm sorry you got fired. I wish I could fix it."

"It can't be fixed. But I still have to figure out how to stop her wedding. Or move it away from the resort, maybe. She was slotted to have her wedding on the beach at noon, but if she moves it to the evening, she'll still be on the premises when the Sanchez raid goes down." The waves rose to her ankles. "I'm afraid for her. She can't be here."

"And you can't be here, either. I can't risk it. You're going to have to play sick for the rest of the weekend and miss the rehearsal dinner."

"What about you?"

"I'll go to the dinner, pass on your regrets, claim I need to stay to look after you. By then, of course, you'll be off the island."

"Of course." Sadness tinged her smile. "And I do feel fairly sick, so it's not a lie."

She glanced at him, something vulnerable in her gaze. "Can I ask how you got hurt?"

"Hurt?"

"Your leg?"

"Oh." She'd noticed that? He hadn't talked about that mission with anyone but the Stryker team, how he'd had to drag Chet out of a terrorist's camp. Chet still kept tabs on his daughter via the CIA. She'd forced him to leave her behind to marry an Iranian prince and become an information asset for the U.S. "I was shot rescuing a friend."

"Are you okay?"

The sweetness in her voice had the power to unravel

him, and he heard the words again. *You're special to me.*
Perhaps she could see that because her smile warmed.
And he couldn't help himself from reaching out then,
touching her face, tucking her hair behind her ear.

"You're so—"

"Scarlett!" The voice rose above the waves and the
call of the gulls. Luke turned, still caught in his words,
now tucked back inside where they belonged. *Beautiful.
You're so beautiful, Scarlett.*

Benito ran toward them. "Oh, I'm so glad I found
you. I don't know what to do."

"What's the matter?" Luke asked, but Benito ignored
him.

"Lucia is missing."

TEN

Despite being a professional, Luke was doing a poor job of hiding his panic over Lucia's disappearance. Scarlett reached out, slid her hand into his and offered a reassuring squeeze.

Somehow over the past hour, she'd suddenly felt as if she and Luke might be a team, in this together. That, when he'd stopped her outside her sister's villa, he had genuinely cared about her and why she'd been crying.

He'd even taken her into his arms, pulled her close. And she'd drunk in his kindness.

He seemed to actually care, those amazing eyes fixed on her as he listened to her words.

As if they mattered.

As if *she* mattered.

"What do you mean she's 'missing?'" Luke asked. Scarlett detected a slight trembling in his voice.

"She was supposed to be trying on her wedding dress, but she—and the dress—are gone," Benito said. "I searched the yacht, but she isn't there, and she isn't in our villa, either. I don't know where she went." Benito shook his head. "You don't think that whoever put that shark in front of our door would really hurt her, do you? I knew I shouldn't have left her alone." He turned to

Scarlett, his eyes dark. "Why did you leave her alone? I thought you were seasick. You don't look seasick."

"I promise, I was sick, Benito," she said, glancing at Luke. He looked angry. She could almost see him rise, draw himself up. Down boy, she tried to communicate with her eyes. "But I'm feeling much better. I just don't have sea legs." She pressed a hand to his arm. "But don't worry, I'll find Lucia. I'll bet it's just prewedding jitters. All brides get them—I promise, it's normal."

Benito put his hands on his hips and looked down at the sand.

"Go back to the yacht and wait for her there. I'll track her down." She glanced at Luke. "I'll see you later, darling."

She turned to leave, but Luke caught her arm and pressed a quick kiss to her cheek. "Be careful."

Oh, she had no doubt that as soon as he could ditch Benito, he'd track them both down.

So where was Lucia?

Prewedding jitters were not likely, because there would be no wedding. But a woman who loved her man —which Lucia clearly did—would want a taste of the happiness she could have had. Especially after trying on her wedding dress.

Scarlett headed up the path to the cabana and recognized a familiar face behind the bar. Raoul looked up and smiled at her as he wiped a glass. *"Hola, señorita."*

"Hello, Raoul. Where's your wedding chapel?"

She should probably know this since she was supposed to be organizing the big day, but she'd been focusing on one crisis at a time. And, well, she'd been let go from her maid-of-honor job, hadn't she?

"I will show you," he said, coming around the bar. He nodded to the other bartender on duty and led the way out of the cabana to a golf cart, motioning for her to hop on.

She slipped onto the bench seat and held the bar as they lurched up the path, past the hotel, to another path on the far side of the resort. Crushed coral lined the pathway to a semi-covered pavilion built into the rock overlooking the ocean. It had seating for perhaps fifty.

And in the arch stood a woman in a wedding dress, facing the sea.

"Thank you, Raoul."

"Anything you need, ma'am," he said. "You want me to wait?"

"I'll take it from here," she said and climbed out.

Yes, she could see herself getting married in this place. The pavilion rose on bamboo pillars, twined with bougainvillea. Instead of a red carpet, sea jewels—washed glass in red and greens—inlaid a path to the altar, the sun slanting through the slats of the open roof.

Lucia didn't turn as Scarlett's flip-flops slapped on the path. Her dress was beautiful with the train fanned out, revealing the scalloped edge, the lacy inset. A halter dress, it buttoned behind her neck, leaving her tanned back open.

She finally sighed and turned. Something about her expression said that she expected someone else.

"It's just me, your maid of honor."

Lucia tried a smile, but it fell and she turned away as Scarlett joined her.

"This is some view." Indeed, waves crashed into the gullies of the cliffs below, the sky endless, cottony clouds hanging over the far horizon. If she spread her arms, she might be able to soar.

"I want to jump," Lucia said. "I want to jump and

forget that I fell in love with a terrorist. That I am going to deceive the man I want to spend my life with."

"You really want to spend your life with Benito?"

Lucia sighed. "A version of him, yes. The kind and gentle man who loves me." She held a bougainvillea blossom. After a moment, she tossed it over the edge. Scarlett watched as it dropped and was engulfed by the waves below. "I didn't expect to fall in love, you know. I expected a monster. I expected him to repulse me. I expected to do a job and leave with my heart intact."

She closed her eyes. "He is not the man I expected. And soon, I found myself not able to pretend anymore."

Not able to pretend anymore.

Scarlett wrapped her arms around herself. "I don't think we can plan out who we'll fall in love with. We just have to be willing to bear the consequences."

"I can't."

Her quiet, even plaintive words speared through Scarlett.

"I love him, Scarlett. This is no longer a game or a mission to me." She turned, her eyes red and full of tears. "This is as close as I will get to my wedding day."

Scarlett slid her arm around Lucia's waist. "I'm sorry."

"I began to believe in the fairy tale. I lied to myself and said that Benito wasn't a killer. That he would never hurt people. And, truthfully, I've never seen him be ruthless or hurt anyone. But how can he be a part of the Sanchez family and not know about their crimes?"

"Maybe he has nothing to do with their crimes."

She sighed. "Even if he doesn't, he will never forgive

me for what I am about to do to his family. A man does not forget betrayal."

Scarlett had nothing to say to that. "Benito is looking for you—"

"Lucia!"

As if saying his name had conjured him, Benito slammed the brakes on his golf cart and jumped out, running through the pavilion. "Why did you run away?"

Luke climbed out, his face taut.

"I didn't run away," Lucia said, clearly trying too hard to add a lightness to her voice. She laughed and it fell flat. "I was just nervous, and I thought if I came here, the fear would go away. And now you've wrecked it, because don't you know it's bad luck to see your bride before the wedding?"

But Benito scooped her up and she laughed. Perhaps only Scarlett saw how she blinked away tears.

This is no longer a game to me.

"Is everything okay?" Luke said, reaching her. He slid his arm around her shoulders.

"Like I said, prewedding jitters," Scarlett said. Luke nodded.

Benito put Lucia down, took her hand and stared out at the ocean. "So, this is where I'll marry my bride. Beautiful." He looked at Luke, as if for confirmation.

"Yes. Of course. But are you talking about Lucia, or the view?"

Benito grinned, kissing Lucia's hand.

"I think you two should get married here, too. The view is too lovely to waste."

Luke managed a smile. Scarlett opened her mouth but nothing emerged.

"See, they are considering it." Benito nodded, a dangerous twinkle in his eyes. "Perhaps we should have a double wedding? Doesn't every woman dream of getting married with her best friend?"

"Oh, no, I…of course, Lucia and I would love to get married together." She glanced at Lucia, who wore an enigmatic smile. "But I need to get married in Minnesota. I can't get married here."

"Why not? Get married now, have your reception in Minnesota."

"I don't have a dress, and besides, my family isn't here."

"That's right, Benito," Lucia said. "Her family isn't here."

Benito pressed another kiss to her hand. "At least you have family. My bride has no one. We must make sure your bridesmaid is here to celebrate with you. No more seasickness. We'll move the rehearsal dinner to the cabana tonight."

Then he bent down and kissed Scarlett's cheek. "Thank you for finding her."

But Scarlett only noticed the keen pressure of Luke's hand on hers. Which probably ended up saving them when a voice shrilled through the pavilion. "What is going on in here?"

Luke looked at her, eyes wide. For a second, she wanted to see if perhaps she could take flight. "Uh…"

Bridgett, now attired in a long, breezy dress, and her two remaining bridesmaids marched down the center aisle, right up to Scarlett. "I thought I told you to stay away from my wedding."

"I…"

"She's not in your wedding," Lucia said, casting Scarlett a look. "She's in mine. She's my maid of honor."

Bridgett glanced at Lucia. "What are you talking about? She's *my* maid of honor."

"No, I'm not," Scarlett said, ignoring the confusion on Bridgett's face. And then something took a hold of her and she said, "I don't even know you."

Bridgett recoiled as if she'd been slapped. "What? You're my sister."

Scarlett frowned and gave thanks for once that she hadn't inherited a drop of Bridgett's beauty. She resembled their Irish mother, thank you very much, with her height issues, her curves, her green eyes and dark unruly hair. "C'mon Lucia, let's get you ready for your party tonight." She reached out her hand.

Benito caught it. "Wait a second here." He turned to Bridgett. "Who are you?"

"I'm Bridgett Hanson. And this is my sister, Scarlett."

Benito raised an eyebrow. "Her sister? What are you doing here?"

"I'm getting married." She looked at Lucia. "What are you doing?"

"I'm getting married, too." Lucia tightened her hold on Scarlett's hand. "Tomorrow night."

"*I'm* getting married tomorrow night. Here."

"I don't think so," Lucia said, glancing at Luke.

"Well, if not here, then somewhere on this resort." Bridgett said. "I am just heading in now to arrange it with the coordinator." She turned to Scarlett. "So, what are you doing here? Why are you with him? What's going on?"

What would a real spy do, or say? What—

"I'm her fiancé. Remember, we met yesterday? In the spa?" Good thing Luke had her hand or she might fall right over.

"Of course I remember you. When did this happen? In the taxi ride to the island?" She turned to Scarlett. "You said you barely knew this guy! What about Dylan?"

Benito's eyes narrowed dangerously.

"Well, see, Luke and I have a sort of on-again, off-again—"

"On-again," he said quickly.

"—relationship."

"Yeah, I surprised her here when I heard she was coming."

"But didn't you and she come for our wedding?" Benito asked.

"We did, but we had a big fight a few weeks ago, and she called it off. So I thought I'd try and see if this romantic setting wouldn't woo her back into my arms." As if to emphasize his words, Luke pulled her into a side embrace. "And it worked."

"There *was* something strange about you two that first night on the yacht," Benito said.

"You spent the night on a yacht with him?"

Scarlett rolled her eyes and didn't even try to defend her virtue to her sister.

"But I don't understand. Whose wedding is she in?" Benito asked.

"Mine!" Bridgett and Lucia chorused.

Oh, boy.

"I don't understand." Benito's tone had a muscle twitching in Luke's jaw. "Do you know her or not?"

That's when the words finally arrived. Scarlett stepped out of Luke's embrace. "Yes, but sometimes I don't want to."

Bridgett's eyes widened, her mouth opening.

"And this entire coincidence is my fault. See, as soon

as I found out about Bridgett's wedding, I told Lucia about the destination on Isla Mujeres—"

"I knew I was here first!" Bridgett said. "I should have the pavilion!"

Scarlett ignored her. "Lucia loved the idea of a destination wedding, although I had no idea that they'd actually pick the same dates. And then, when Bridgett fired me as maid of honor—"

"She fired you?" Benito said.

"Twice. So I thought it wouldn't be a problem for me to attend your wedding, but then Bridgett needed me again, so I thought I'd just attend both—"

"As the maid of honor?"

"What can I say? I'm popular."

She didn't miss Luke's smile. And it sent warmth through her, emboldened her.

"I'm sorry for the mix-up. But don't worry, Benito, I'm fired again, so I'll be here for Lucia. Right by her side the entire time."

Luke's smile vanished as a slow grin slid over Benito's face. "So, this *is* your sister!"

Perhaps he'd been in the sun too long?

"You can get married!"

"Married?" Bridgett asked.

"Married?" Lucia said, her eyebrow rising.

"Married?" Scarlett echoed.

"Yes. Right here, tomorrow, beside Lucia."

Luke's arm tightened around her.

"I can't think of any reason why not, can you?" Benito asked.

Luke's mouth opened yet nothing came out.

Scarlett couldn't work with nothing.

"Then it's a double wedding." He leaned down, kissed

Scarlett on the cheek, then clamped Luke on the arm. "C'mon, Luke. Let's get you a suit."

Luke looked hard at Scarlett and she managed a smile and a nod.

"You're getting married?" Bridgett asked, her gaze going between Lucia and Scarlett.

"Huh. Yeah. I don't suppose you want to be my maid of honor?"

Luke looked like an albatross. He stared at himself in the mirror in Benito's bedroom on the yacht and realized he'd lost his mind.

For a second, when he saw his reflection, clad in a white suit, a gray ascot at his neck, shaven and showered, he actually saw himself standing at the altar, watching his bride—his bride?—walk down the aisle.

He imagined Scarlett's dark caramel hair piled high on her head, tendrils curling around her face, those big green eyes pinned on him, as if he might actually be her hero.

How he suddenly wanted to be, wanted to rescue her from this mess he'd created. Fired, again, from her crazy sister's wedding. Roped, one wrong word at a time, into danger, and now cajoled into marrying him.

Except he wouldn't let it get that far. No, he'd come up with a plan, something to oust her from the wedding, off the island and preferably out of Mexico.

A doozy of a fight should do it, although the ideas that entered his brain made him a little sick.

"The suit is a good fit. Perhaps a little wide around the waist." Benito sat at his bar, nursing a drink, as his valet tried to fit Luke into Benito's clothes. "But trust me, she'll only see you."

The guy who should have been her date? Or the guy

who had dragged her into trouble? Who would Scarlett see?

"Benito, are you really sure this a good idea? I mean, maybe she's not ready."

"She said yes, correct?"

Yes? To what? To his mythical wedding proposal? He nodded.

"And you wouldn't ask her to marry you if you weren't ready, correct?"

Luke managed a smile.

"So, why wait? Do you love her?"

Did he love her? He nodded, but the words cut inside him. He loved the way she laughed, her eyes lighting up her entire face. He loved her spontaneity, the way she could keep up with his stories and add to them. He loved her willingness to help Lucia, and even her sister.

He loved the way she listened to him without judgment. And how she yielded in his arms.

And he loved the way she'd given him her secrets, looking at him with trust in her eyes.

Most of all, he loved how…how he trusted her back.

Yes, a part of him, the part that didn't live in a crazy world of danger and lies, the part that wanted to be just her wedding date, could easily love her.

"Of course I do," he added to his nod.

Benito smiled. "The first time I met Lucia, I knew she would be my wife. She saw a good man in me. A man I wanted to be. She makes me feel like I am that man." He stared out the window. "I would kill for her."

Cold streaked down Luke's spine at Benito's words, but he just kept staring at his reflection. Suddenly, he wished he could go back to that moment when Scarlett opened his taxi door. He should have taken one extra second to ask, to confirm. *Are you Stacey?*

When she said no, he should have pushed her out of the taxi.

He raised his gaze, met Benito's in the mirror. "Me, too. Scarlett makes me feel like I'm the man I should be."

Benito nodded and took a drink.

Yes, tonight, somehow, Luke would have to make a spectacle to make sure Scarlett hadn't a prayer of attending tomorrow's wedding. Or…

Plead with her to dump him. Publicly.

Both options made his chest clench.

"I need to find a wedding ring," he said, leaving the suit in Benito's care. Benito gave him a strange smile as Luke left the yacht and headed down the dock, hoping to find Scarlett and Lucia.

He'd left them alone long enough. Yes, Scarlett had the pager, but without him nearby, it would offer little in the way of rescue. If either of them got hurt, he'd never forgive himself.

Not that he ever forgave himself. He just piled his mistakes on top of each other. *You need to forgive yourself, Luke.*

Scarlett's words from last night wound through him. As did his retort, *I can't erase what happened.*

No, his mistakes still woke him in a cold sweat.

If only he hadn't been so thirsty for a woman's laughter, her touch. Her acceptance. And that only made his realization worse. He *was* like his father. A person who let his emptiness destroy the lives of others. His father went from woman to woman, shattering their hearts, and eventually their family.

I keep waiting for Him to betray me, to walk away.

When he'd spoken those words in the darkness on the boat, he'd meant them to be about God, but they could apply to his father, too. He couldn't believe he'd actually said that, had actually let her that far inside. Thankfully, she'd been gentle. *God isn't like your father, Luke.*

If he'd never forgiven his father, how could he possibly forgive himself for being just like him?

He doesn't treat us as we think we should be treated. He wanted to flinch at the quiet accuracy of her statement. He couldn't bear to trust God's love—His forgiveness—for him. Not after his sins.

Which meant that even if he did want to imagine Scarlett in a white dress, her eyes shining as she looked at him, as she walked down the aisle, he had to purge that thought from his mind and thank God that this gig was temporary.

He could love Scarlett. In fact, he might be halfway there already.

But he didn't deserve her. He didn't deserve to be happy.

Sweat filmed his spine as he passed by the cabana and cut through the open-air bar to catch some shade.

Bridgett sat at a high-top table alone, nursing some orange drink, her blond hair piled high on her head. With her regal cheekbones and full lips, he could see her on a cover of a magazine or strutting down some runway. Suddenly he veered toward her, something hot sizzling in his chest.

"I just have to tell you something," he said, his voice apparently running the show, the tone dark and angry.

Bridgett looked up. Her eyes were red-rimmed. That might have told him something, might have sent off a warning, but he flew right past that.

"Your sister is amazing. She's funny and brave and

compassionate, but you don't see that, do you? You see the kid sister who divided your family, but you don't see what it cost her. She dropped everything to come down here and help you plan your wedding, and you're firing her because of a mistake the chef made—"

"Duncan was in love with her." Bridgett's words, so softly spoken, stopped him cold. She ran her finger around the rim of her glass. "He just never had the courage to ask her out. But he did love her, and I stole him." She looked up at Luke, and her eyes filled. "I stole him because I hated her. I'm not even sure why, but I blamed her for the fact that my parents always ran back and forth between us."

Luke inhaled slowly, still trying to believe her words. "It's because you felt guilty. And you hated that feeling. So you hated her." He wasn't exactly sure where that came from, but it felt right.

"Yeah." She pressed her manicured fingers to her face. "I never dreamed that one agent meeting in Minneapolis would lead to so many sacrifices. Yes, a part of me loved being in the limelight. But I never expected it, and I walked into it without realizing the cost. For a long while, I thought that being in front of the camera was where I belonged, but you know, it blinds you. You always see yourself through the lens of others until... until you don't know who you are. Until you don't know yourself at all."

Luke rested his foot on a rung of the high-top chair. "Why did you come to Rochester?"

She stared at her drink. "I fell in love with the wrong man." She closed her eyes. "He was a photographer, and he made me feel beautiful. I don't know why I needed his love so much, but I ate up his words as if I'd been starving for years. He told me that he wanted to marry me."

Luke knew the rest but waited for it anyway, a fist tightening in his gut.

"But he was already married."

Yes, that might cause someone to move across the ocean and find a life in a different town. Like Rochester.

Like Prague.

"I'm sorry," he said. "But that doesn't give you an excuse to hurt your sister. Or marry a man you don't love."

"But I do love Duncan. See, I started out wanting to hurt my sister for her perfect, easy life. For taking my parents from me. But then I fell in love." She looked up at Luke, her eyes glossy again. "I love him more than I ever dreamed. He's solid and kind and he doesn't see me through a lens. Duncan doesn't need me to be any more than I am. He sees me without makeup and with all my blemishes and loves me anyway."

"But he loved Scarlett."

She drew in a breath. "I thought, when she confessed that she loved him at my engagement party, that he'd dump me and run back to her. So I cut her out of my life and shamed her."

"She loves you, Bridgett. You underestimate her. She came here with a full heart to help you. I think she wants you to be happy."

Bridgett looked up at him. "I guess I don't deserve her."

Well, that made two of them.

"I even set her up on a blind date this weekend with one of Duncan's geeky cousins. I called it a favor. But really, I just wanted to pour salt in the wound. Who knew that she was already engaged? I can't believe it—you two are really getting married? Tomorrow?"

And if he said no, then what? Scarlett would probably end up on the arm of Dylan from Davenport, dumped yet again.

So he said it with conviction, with so much of his heart in the words, for Scarlett and her honor. "Yes. I'm marrying your sister tomorrow at sunset."

She narrowed her eyes at him. "I barely know you. Can I have your word that you won't hurt her? Won't betray her in any way?"

He dug deep and found a smile that didn't belong to him, a voice that he didn't own, and said, "Yes. You have my word." And he knew that there would never be forgiveness for him.

ELEVEN

"You are so beautiful."

The words out of the salesclerk's mouth didn't have the impact that they might have if issued from Luke, but Scarlett would embrace them, because yes, she looked beautiful. She stood in her so-called wedding dress on the tiny platform that elevated her above the floor, her reflection captured in three giant mirrors that revealed all sides of her dress, as well as Lucia, seated in the viewing chairs, a grin on her face.

"I'm not getting married, you know," Scarlett said when the salesclerk stepped away. Although as soon as she ventured into the tiny boutique of all-occasion dresses—including spur-of-the-moment wedding dresses—a switch flipped inside her brain. She started smelling flowers and hearing dance music, and she saw in her mind's eye Luke standing at the end of the aisle, grinning at her.

Her groom.

No, not her groom!

"It's all pretend, let's not forget that."

Lucia made a face, got up and straightened the train. The dress had a fairy-tale aura about it with tiny capped sleeves, a row of pearl buttons up the back, layers of ruffles that spilled down the train. "Well, you should be. The way Luke looks at you—if I didn't know it was all for my benefit, I would buy that you two were madly in love."

Well, one of them might be. Wait, no. Had she really thought that? She didn't love Luke. She barely knew him. Sure, he'd come after her, listened to her, and yes, when he looked at her she could believe that she just might be the only girl on the planet. But she needed to focus on the word *pretend*. Fake. For the benefit of the mission.

"He's a good actor."

"Apparently, so are you."

Scarlett averted her face before Lucia spotted the truth. She could love Luke Dekker. She could quit her job—not that she had a real one—and move across the ocean with him to Prague, to start a new life. She saw herself—foolishly, she knew that—becoming his partner, maybe going undercover again, a new identity every weekend.

The ultimate temp job.

I think you have a lot of heroine inside of you.

She hated how she nearly gulped those words whole, letting them nourish her.

Luke made her feel like the main attraction, not an afterthought.

And standing here in the perfect dress didn't quelch that feeling, not at all.

The perfect—oh, no! "I have to call the airport and make sure my sister's dress has arrived. And I have to find a new location for her wedding." She turned her back to Lucia. "Will you unzip me?" Then, to the saleslady, "I'll take it."

"Very good. Shall I have it steamed and sent to your hotel?"

"Yes, please." And then, before Lucia could step in and put it on Benito's account, she pulled out her credit card.

Maybe she'd simply have the hotel ship it home. A souvenir.

Lucia gave her a small smile as Scarlett signed the sales slip. "Where do people get married on this island, ma'am, other than the resorts?"

"Oh, on the North Beach, of course. And at the lighthouse on the point at the south end of the island. It's a lovely place for a wedding."

"Thank you." She grabbed Lucia's hand. "C'mon. We've got work to do."

"What are we doing?"

"I can't have my sister getting married at the resort. Not with...well, with the fireworks planned. We're planning a new wedding, Lucia. And it all starts will my pal Raoul."

She found him sweeping the walkway outside the resort. "I need your help, Raoul."

"Anything for you, *señorita*."

She just loved how he said that.

Of course, planning Bridgett's new wedding only stirred her own fairy tale inside, from the flowers to the cake to the musicians to the candles that would light the path up to the lighthouse.

She made a point of checking out the view, standing at the pinnacle of the south-facing cliffs, again feeling as if she could soar.

"It's even more beautiful than the view at the pavilion," Lucia said.

"I hope Bridgett agrees. The reception yacht can pick them up at the landing below, and hopefully Raoul has lined up the limousines."

"Yeah, all two that are on the island."

"There aren't that many guests, so maybe they can take cabs, too. But I want the wedding party to go over in the limos before the CIA shows up."

Lucia's smile fell.

"Sorry."

"No. It's good for me to remember that despite all the fuss, there will be no wedding."

There would be no wedding for either of them.

"I don't understand. Why are you doing all this for your sister? I met her—she isn't very…"

"It's okay." Scarlett took the path up to the lighthouse, making a mental note for the florist as to where to assemble the bougainvillea arch. "Bridgett and I used to be close, but something changed when she left home to model. At first I blamed it on her busy life, but after that I decided that she just wasn't the same person. She was who they wanted her to be. I'd lost her. I guess a part of me wants to believe she's still there, that she knows that I love her, despite her changes. She's not an afterthought to me. She's a big deal."

"That's very noble."

Was it?

"Well, there's another part, too. See, I sort of made a spectacle at her engagement party. I accused her of stealing my boyfriend. Which of course she didn't, but it felt like it. But it made me realize that he didn't love me. At least not enough to come after me. I guess that's what I'm holding out for—the guy who will come after me."

"Benito tracked me down after meeting me at a diplomatic reception. He waited in the lobby the next day for two hours with lilies until I passed through. I had planned on making an impact, but I have to admit, I didn't expect to be wooed by him so easily."

"You weren't an afterthought to him. You are a big deal."

Lucia smiled, an expression on her face that made Scarlett want to weep. She put her arm around Lucia's tanned shoulders as they walked back to the golf cart.

By the time they returned for the rehearsal dinner, the sun had just begun to set over the resort, the palm trees inky brushes against the painted sky. They cast tufted shadows upon the lawn, and the orange-streaked sunset turned the water to burning coals. Scarlett stood on the outskirts of the pavilion and listened to the priest Benito and Lucia had hired walk them through the steps. Then, Scarlett lined up with Benito's best man, slipped her arm through his and imagined it might be Luke.

But Luke stood at the back of the pavilion, saying little. He left before the rehearsal ended.

"See you at dinner," Lucia said after Scarlett walked back to her yacht with Benito.

Scarlett then spent a good half hour bemoaning her Minnesota wardrobe. She'd packed her only little black dress, a number she usually wore with a white blouse. But at least the color enhanced yesterday's tan. She twisted up her hair, added a pink coral necklace and slipped into a pair of heels. Not necessarily beachwear, but it would have to do.

Of course, Luke would look like a model straight out of a magazine with his burnished gold hair, those light brown eyes that missed nothing. Probably he'd smell good, too. She added a little lipstick and perfume and told herself again this wasn't a date.

Then, she made her way to the dinner.

Her sister had actually booked the deck restaurant

in the hotel for her rehearsal dinner. Music drifted out from the party, the deck lit by lanterns and luminaries. Scarlett had sent Bridgett a note via Raoul about the change of wedding ceremony venues. The fact that she hadn't shown up at the pavilion during rehearsal to duke it out with Lucia seemed a sign of success. Hopefully, Bridgett had a beautiful sunset rehearsal at the lighthouse.

God, please bless her party, her wedding. Yes, she would like to show Bridgett that she endorsed her marriage, that she hoped Bridgett and Duncan lived happily ever after.

Really.

And if they listened to her, they actually *would* live happily ever after.

She cut down the path to the cabana at the beach, where lights strung between palm trees twinkled against the night, where luminarias glowed to light the path toward the thatched-roof picnic shelter. The spice of the grill lured her in to stand at the edge of the wooden floor where Lucia and Benito danced the salsa.

She couldn't dance.

Hopefully, Luke wouldn't ask.

"Wow, you look beautiful."

Coming from his lips, the words took away her breath. She turned and Luke stood there, wearing a white shirt, a pair of black linen pants.

He held out his hand. "Care to dance?"

"I…I don't know how, Luke. I can't dance the salsa."

He gave her a soft, playful smile. Oh, her romantic heart didn't stand a chance.

The song ended, the music changing beat. "This is a waltz. Just take my hand and hold on."

"I've pretty much been doing that since we met in the cab." Oh, for goodness' sake. But he grinned at her and led her to the dance floor. "It's a three-count. One-two-three, one-two-three. Start by stepping back with your right foot, and I'll take it from there."

Ho-kay.

She stumbled, and he caught her. "Relax."

Relax. With his hand on her upper back, holding her? But as she breathed out, she relished the safety of his arms.

They started again and she counted out her steps, stiff, jerky.

"Close your eyes."

"What?"

"You're trying to lead. I get that—most women are worried that we men are going to lead you someplace bad—into the chairs, or the sand. But I promise to take care of you. Close your eyes."

"Okay."

Then, magic happened. She stopped worrying about the steps and just let him lead her, gently, easily around the dance floor, keeping the beat, safe in his arms.

Around and around, one-two-three until she became the music and lost herself.

It ended too soon. She opened her eyes, expecting to see him smile.

But he almost seemed in pain, his eyes dark. "I'm so sorry, Scarlett, for what I'm about to do."

Then he backed away from her, and in a voice that didn't seem to belong to the man she'd come to know, a voice that he must have conjured, said, "Why didn't you tell me you were still in love with your old boyfriend?"

Oh, please, let this be fake. She couldn't bear the

thought that all the rest had been pretend and this, this man who spat out venom, might be real.

Might be the true Luke Dekker.

Because this wasn't the man she'd fallen in love with at all.

"My old boyfriend? What do you mean I'm still in love with my old boyfriend?" Her voice emerged as if through broken glass, halting, crisp.

He knew it would hurt her, knew that dragging up Duncan would only make it personal, make her react with real emotions.

Real hurt.

Real betrayal.

But hopefully those real emotions would also convince Benito, and send her packing from Lucia's wedding tomorrow.

So he went for the jugular, despite the fact that the look on her face could tear him in half. "Yeah, your *boyfriend,* Duncan. The guy I just ran into, the one who told me he wants you back. That he is *still in love with you.*"

"But…Duncan never loved me—"

"Not like me, of course. But there is no figuring out love, is there, baby?" He raised his voice and cast his gaze around the crowd. *C'mon Scarlett, play along.*

She backed away from him, her mouth opening, her face white. "I…when did he tell you this?"

Oh, no, she didn't really believe him, did she?

"Earlier today, while you were out buying your wedding dress. I ran into him, and we had a little heart-to-heart. He told me how your sister stole him away from you, but how he's come to his senses. How he loves you and wants you back. But you already knew that, didn't you?"

Her eyes widened and he hated the lie. And the fact he told it so convincingly. But great lies were built on truths. He'd just changed the name Bridgett to Duncan.

Still, the fact that Duncan had loved her hadn't been a lie, and he didn't know exactly how he felt about the fact that the guy might indeed still carry a torch for the girl he...

Loved. Oh, no. He'd been dodging that truth all day but he finally landed on the emotion bubbling inside. Love. He loved Scarlett. And he was about to eviscerate her in public. "And, according to Duncan, you love him, too. You even tried to break up your sister's wedding to prove it." Please, don't flinch, Scarlett.

He forced himself not to look away, despite the look on her face.

"But...I don't love Duncan."

"Please. He's here, on the island."

"Well, of course he is, but—"

"And earlier today you were in his villa, when you should have been home, seasick."

"What? I was—"

"I don't want to hear any more. Just stop with the lies, Scarlett. I thought we had something. I thought—" and he didn't want to admit it, but this part came right from the real Luke Dekker—"I thought we really had something that we could build on. I saw our future in your eyes, and I knew that you were the only person I would ever risk being with." Could he say the next part? "And now...you destroyed that."

Her eyes filled, her hand pressed to her mouth. She shook her head, almost pleading, and with everything inside him he wanted to yank back his words. But he had to seal the deal.

For Scarlett's sake.

For Lucia's sake.

For the sake of the mission.

It would help, however, if Scarlett confessed, even played along.

"I'm sorry I ever met you," he said, dropping his voice to a growl. "I'm sorry I ever loved you." He swallowed hard, then spit the last words out, hating himself. "You weren't worth my time."

Something flashed in her eyes then.

And the Scarlett he knew, the Scarlett he loved, the woman he'd just decimated, came to life.

"Yeah, well, me too, jack."

Atta girl.

"Because you're nothing but a fake."

Except her words, her tone, the glisten of her eyes looked real. Too real.

"You're just a man who speaks out both sides of his mouth. A liar."

Watch it now, Scarlett. Be careful. But she was so terribly right, her words landing like a blade in his heart.

"I do love Duncan! I always have, and I should have figured out that this thing with you was just a fling. I...*hate* you. I'm so glad I finally figured that out." She lifted her gaze to the onlookers, gathering courage. "You'd end up cheating on me with a bridesmaid anyway."

Ow. Okay, that hurt.

"And I wouldn't marry you if...if you were the last man on this island."

Then she turned and found Lucia in the crowd. "I'm

sorry, Lucia, I can't stay. I hope Benito turns out to be a better groom than this jerk."

"Good riddance," Luke said quietly as Scarlett gave him one last look, shook her head and left the dance floor.

Mission accomplished.

Except, oh, how he wanted to run after her, grab her arm, whirl her around and pull her into his arms. *I'm sorry, Scarlett.*

I'm sorry.

He saw Claudio's eyes on him as he turned away from her.

"So, she cheated on you this morning, while she was playing seasick?" Benito slipped up beside him, clamped a hand on his shoulder.

"Looks like it," Luke choked out. Scarlett had reached the edge of the light and was now disappearing into the darkness.

"Sorry, Luke. C'mon, I'll buy you a drink."

But Luke didn't want a drink. Everything he thirsted for he'd just pushed out of his life. And, given the way he'd used her own pain against her, he had no doubts she'd never want to talk to him again.

Benito walked him to the bar where Luke ordered a Coke.

"You don't want anything stronger?" Benito asked.

"No. I don't want to track down Duncan and hurt him."

"Maybe the guys and I should do it for you."

Luke shook his head. "If she wants him, she can have him."

"Just like that, you're going to give her up? No fight?" Lucia came to the bar and slid onto a bench. He frowned at her. She, better than anyone, had to know that he'd made up the entire spectacle.

"What do you expect me to do?"

"Run after her. Let her explain. Tell her that you love her anyway." She glanced at Benito, then back to Luke. "That's what love does. It hopes and believes in a logical explanation. And it forgives."

Had Lucia lost her mind? She wasn't seriously suggesting...or, maybe this had more to do with her own pain than Scarlett's. Still, they had to stick to the script. He gave her a dark look. Pay attention, Lucia. "I can't forgive this."

"Then you never really loved her, man," Benito said, raising an eyebrow. "You didn't even let her explain."

Lucia smiled at him, her eyes glowing, clearly ignoring Luke's silent warnings.

"Let's go find her, see if she has anything to say." Benito hooked his hand around Luke's neck. What could he do?

Please, Scarlett, be furious. Refuse to take me back. "But you're at your rehearsal dinner."

"Hey. We men have to stick together. Besides, my bride isn't so sure this isn't your fault. Are you, darling?"

Sure enough, Lucia looked at him as if she wanted to take a piece out of him. "Find her."

His lips tightened to a grim line. She met his eyes without a blink.

He simply didn't understand women. Didn't Lucia know that if she and Scarlett showed up tomorrow, either—or both—of them could get hurt? He simply couldn't protect them both.

"Who says I want her back?"

"Do you love her?" Benito asked for the second time in less than two days.

Luke stared out into the darkness at the path she'd taken, seeing her face, the way tears pooled in her eyes…

"Let's go." Benito grabbed his arm, practically yanking him from the bar. They hiked across the dance floor, leaving the glow of the party, heading across the sand. Waves chased them on the shore, the music drifting on the breeze. The smell of the ocean called to him. Run.

"Who is this Duncan guy?" Benito asked.

"He's from back home. They had a thing for a couple years. Then her sister came into the picture. He fell for the sister—"

"And dumped Scarlett? What was he thinking?"

Good question, except, Duncan clearly *hadn't* been thinking. A guy who hadn't even had the guts to ask Scarlett out on a real date didn't deserve her. Add to that the fact that he let her twist in the wind for so long and didn't even come clean after she'd embarrassed herself at the engagement dinner. Yeah, Luke would like to straighten out Duncan a little. "I don't know. But more importantly, she isn't over him."

"She's over him. She just needs to let go of the past and see what she has in front of her."

Luke glanced at him.

"You, man." Benito rolled his eyes. "Wow. It's a good thing I'm making you get married tomorrow, or I'm not sure you'd *ever* tie the knot."

That, actually, was completely accurate.

They cut past the cabana toward the hotel. "There she is."

Indeed. Scarlett stood outside the cabana, near the pool…talking to another man.

And even though Luke knew he'd spun the entire tale, even though he knew—or felt pretty sure that he knew—that Scarlett didn't love him, it still jolted him to see her reach out and take the man's hand and smile up at him.

He reached out and wiped away a tear from her face.

Then he pulled her into a hug, her arms reaching around his neck.

No…it couldn't be. Duncan?

She didn't *really* want Duncan back, did she?

Luke froze, unable to move. She *had* come to Cancun to break up her sister's wedding.

"I'm going to kill him," Luke said. But Benito beat him to the punch—literally. Luke didn't stop Benito as he cut across the patio on a path of destruction toward Duncan.

Maybe he should have. Yes, for sure he should have. Luke should have never let Benito grab Scarlett's arm and tear her away from Duncan's embrace.

He should have jumped in to stop him before Benito pulled back and slammed his fist square in Duncan's face.

Oops.

TWELVE

This game had stopped being pretend and turned into full, bloody reality. Maybe it had been reality all along and now it had simply spilled over into Scarlett's real life.

Her Minnesota life.

Duncan's life.

"Duncan!" The poor man looked up at her, holding his nose, blood dribbling down his chin. He'd never been the bodybuilder type—he was more of the coffee-shop-and-philosophy brand of man, with unremarkable hair, round spectacles and soft hands. To see him prone on the patio, blinking up at her as if he'd been attacked by a buffalo...her heart went out to him.

She rounded on Luke. "What was that for?"

Luke held up his hands. "I didn't hit him."

True. She growled at Benito. "Why did you do that?"

Benito stood over Duncan, his fist clenched. Duncan just pinched his bloody nose. "He's trying to steal you. From Luke."

Oh, for cryin' in the sink, she wasn't a puppy. Or a priceless diamond. And, in case he hadn't noticed, "Luke broke up with *me*. He doesn't want me back."

"That's a lie. He loves you." Benito glanced at Luke, who nodded.

What?

Then why the big—and painful, she might add—break up at the rehearsal dinner?

Every accusation he'd hurled at her dug another piece out of her, made her want to curl into a ball, put her hands over her head.

You weren't worth my time. That line was delivered like a fist in the gut and she still ached from the blow, the words ringing in her head even with the knowledge that he'd most likely been lying.

Probably.

She hoped.

Oh, it didn't matter anyway, because Luke had done what he'd intended. He'd broken up with her. Publicly. So he wouldn't have to marry her tomorrow.

No, no, so she would be safe when Lucia didn't marry Benito tomorrow.

She'd had a difficult time keeping that at the forefront of her brain as she'd stalked away from the dinner, as she wiped her hands across her eyes, as she'd nearly plowed right into Duncan.

"Whoa—hey, what—Scarlett, is that you?" Duncan's kind voice had cut through her dark thoughts, her plan to run back to her hotel room and bury her head in her pillow and weep. He gripped her by her bare shoulders and leaned down to peer at her face. "Are you crying?"

She had been. And she'd had no defense as she cleared her tears.

"I just broke up with my fiancé." It was part pride, part charade that formed those words, especially since Bridgett had most likely filled him in on her engagement.

"Your *fiancé?* What? Since when are you engaged?"

Or not. She shook her head. "It's a long story, Duncan."

"I wouldn't mind listening. You used to share your thoughts with me."

"That was a long time ago."

He looked down, away from her. "Probably too long. Listen, we can talk if you want. The rehearsal is over, the party's in full swing. I came back to get Bridgett's sandals. Her feet hurt." He gave a small smile. "It was awfully nice of you to change the venue. Bridgett loves the lighthouse."

He averted his eyes again when he said it, and that's when she grabbed his arm and brought him off the pathway toward the pool.

"I'm so sorry that I embarrassed you the night of the engagement dinner, Duncan. I was hurt, and I dreamed up this future with you—"

"It's my fault."

"No, really. I should have figured out that you weren't in love with me—"

"But, Scarlett, I was."

And that had silenced her, stealing the words right out of her mind, stilling the crazy emotions swirling in her chest.

"What?"

He looked away. "Yeah. I was in love with you for two years. But I didn't have the courage to tell you. And then your sister showed up and she…well, she made it so easy. She asked me out, and she asked me to marry her."

Her sister had done the proposing? Not Duncan?

"Do you…love her?"

He gave her a smile. "I'm crazy about her. But you weren't wrong. I was a coward with you. Then…and when you said something at the engagement party. I told your sister the truth that night, and amazingly, she still wanted me." He shook his head. "I'm so sorry you got caught in the middle of this. That I hurt you."

"You…loved me? And you never told me? You let me believe we were just friends? Why?"

"Because I couldn't believe that you would want me." He gave a self-deprecating laugh.

"Oh, Duncan. The crazy lives we lead by not telling the truth." She took a breath, and for a second her own crazy truth sizzled at the tip of her lips. *I'm not really engaged.* But she couldn't betray Luke's secret. Not without jeopardizing Lucia and Luke's safety.

And, after all their sacrifices, all the hurt, it remained the one thing they had together.

"Can you forgive me?" Duncan asked.

She gave him a small smile and took his hand. "Of course. As long as you promise to take good care of my sister."

"I promise." Then he'd leaned down, wrapped his arms around her and drawn her into a brotherly embrace.

She'd slipped her arms around his neck. So comfortable, so familiar and…she felt nothing.

Nothing remained of the feelings, the wild crush she'd had on Duncan, except a gentle, warm affection.

Most of all, her crush hadn't compared in the least to the swirl of feelings she had for Luke.

And she'd known Duncan for two years. Luke, for two days.

Duncan's cowardice had saved her from a life of humdrum.

Not that she'd necessarily have a life of excitement—or of any kind—with Luke, but knowing the difference mattered. At least now, she knew what she wanted.

Luke.

And then, as if by thinking his name, she'd conjured his voice.

"I'm going to kill him."

Huh? She let go just as Benito grabbed her arm, ripping her away from Duncan. She'd barely found her footing when Benito sent his fist into poor, unarmed, peace-loving Duncan's face.

Duncan slammed into the pavement.

She looked now at Luke, Benito's words vibrating in her head.

"You love me?"

Luke met her eyes with a raw expression. The look of someone unmasked. His mouth opened, but for the first time, nothing of his fast-talking wit emerged.

Luke *loved* her? No, it had to be a part of the game. But they'd had their goodbye, their explosive parting. Why would he track her down unless…

Benito didn't believe them. Or maybe he did and simply wanted to do a good deed. One that Luke couldn't stop.

Then why didn't she see a warning in his eyes instead? Why the emotion, the…fear? The silence?

She glanced at Duncan, now leaning his head back, checking the bleeding. "Benito, let him up."

She reached out and helped Duncan to his feet, scrambling for words. She and Luke couldn't kiss and make up because then she had no doubt that she *would* be getting married tomorrow night.

Besides, she had to save Duncan from another right hook. And try to get her scrambled thoughts in order.

"Why don't we all cool off a bit…"

"Do you love him or not?" Benito demanded.

"Duncan or Luke?"

Benito looked as if he just might hit her. "Luke."

"Of course I love Luke." And then, because he'd gone first, and because she just had to make sure, she let him see her love right there in her eyes.

It seemed to strip something from him, and he looked away.

Good. She shouldn't be the only one scrambling to figure out what to do. But he could back her up anytime here.

"I wasn't trying to steal her, for pity's sake!" Duncan had finally stopped the bleeding and now rounded on Benito, as if he might strike him back. Except he stood a good three inches shorter and had to glare up at Benito.

She would have laughed but she wanted to give Duncan props. The poor man was probably quoting Bible verses in his head. *Yea, though I walk through the valley of the shadow of death, I will not fear…*

"You weren't? You're not here to take her away from Luke?" Benito said.

"I'm standing right here, Benito. And last time I looked, I wasn't for sale."

But Benito ignored her. As did Duncan.

"Of course not. I'm marrying her sister tomorrow. I don't want Scarlett."

Ouch. That could have come out nicer.

"She's just a friend."

Better, but still. Ow.

Benito narrowed his eyes at Duncan. "You weren't in love with her?"

Duncan drew in a breath. "I was. But not anymore."

She could feel Luke's exhale of relief from a foot away.

The argument had been a farce. He didn't really believe that she loved Duncan.

Not everyone is like that woman who lied to you.

It seemed she wasn't the only one struggling to part fact from fantasy.

Benito smiled. "See, Luke? I told you that it would work out."

"Yeah, you were right, dude." But his eyes widened when Benito clamped him on the shoulder.

"Tomorrow, there will be two weddings."

Do. Something. She saw it in Luke's face when he glanced at her, and despite the screaming inside, despite the fact that yes, she would love to see Luke's eyes when she showed up in that dress and that she longed to tell him that she would never betray him, never lie to him, she said, quietly, "No."

Benito frowned at her. "What?"

"No. Luke doesn't trust me. And I refuse to marry a man who doesn't trust me. It's over, Benito." Then without another word, she broke through the huddle of men and walked toward her hotel.

Halfway up the path, she hazarded a look over her shoulder. Duncan had vanished, and Luke and Benito had turned down the pathway back toward the beach party.

No one was coming after her.

"Yes, I took care of it, Chet." Luke sat on his bed in the darkness of his villa, his cell phone pressed to his ear, the doors to his balcony open. The scent of a storm was in the air, the smell of seaweed and other debris tossed to shore. Below his balcony, the waves pounded the coral, hollowing out the rock.

"Scarlett won't be in the way tomorrow? Because you need to focus all your energy on Lucia. Man, I wish you had waited for Stacey."

Him, too. Except, well, then he wouldn't have met Scarlett and…no, no, that would have been better, too—

"I can't do anything about it now. And I'll be ready in the morning. Just tell me where you want me." He imagined that Chet had met the other members of the assault team, briefing them and working with the commander of the CIA to create their plan of attack. The pictures Luke had sent earlier of the wedding pavilion and the cliffs should help the team lay out a strategy. At least he hadn't screwed up that part.

He loves you, Benito had said, and why, why, why had he nodded? And worse, for a brief second, when she looked at him, she'd caught him with all his emotions on the surface, the truth right there for her to see. Which had turned him lethally mute. Thankfully, she thought fast on her feet. She'd saved both their hides.

"We need visual confirmation of Augusto, so as soon as Lucia signals that he's arrived, you let me know. You still have your earpiece?"

Luke braced his forehead on his hand. *Of course I love Luke.* That had sounded so real, her eyes matching her words. Wow, she had pulled this charade off in spades.

"Luke?"

"Yeah. I got it. Sorry."

"Is your head in this game?"

Luke stood up and leaned on the dresser, peering at himself in the mirror. Mildly burned, a growth of whiskers, his eyes red from the glare of the sun, he looked like a guy hanging out at a yacht club instead of on security detail.

Head in the game. Head in the game. "Yes. Absolutely."

"Okay. I'm trusting you. You're the only eyes I have, so be ready. We don't want to have to wait until the bride is at the altar—that only makes her a target."

"Got it. I'll be in touch as soon as I see him."

"Be safe." Chet clicked off and Luke tossed his cell phone on the desk.

Luke doesn't trust me. And I refuse to marry a man who doesn't trust me.

He needed to purge those words from his chest where they burned a hole through him and threatened to turn him inside out.

He did trust her.

He trusted her because…because that's what you did when you loved someone. Even if they don't deserve it—which she did—you trusted them because the alternative would haunt you, tear you to shreds.

"I'm sorry, Scarlett," he said. Maybe after…well, he'd like to track her down. Take her out on a real date.

Although he doubted that she would speak to him again.

He walked out to the balcony and stood at the rail, listening to the black sea.

"Hello, Luke."

Everything inside him tensed. He schooled his voice. "Claudio. Should I ask what you're doing in my villa?"

Claudio sat in a chair, staring out at the ocean. Only

the orange ash of his cigarette glowed in the darkness and betrayed his face. Luke replayed his conversation with Chet in his head. How much had Claudio heard? "Who were you talking to?"

"A friend. I have a surprise planned for Scarlett tomorrow. I'm going to try and get her back." Too much of that lie was salted with truth.

"Now, that's the thing. I don't think you two were ever engaged. That you even knew each other before this weekend. Sure, you care about her, but she looks at you with surprise. Like she can't believe you walked into her life."

Uh-oh.

"And frankly, you look at her the same way."

He did? So, some things he couldn't hide. "I'm always amazed that I lucked out with such an incredible woman."

"You're lying. You're here for some other reason."

"Like what?"

"To hurt my family. I'm not sure why I think that, but you watch everything, Luke. Like a professional. And you're always hovering around Benito. Keep your friends close, your enemies closer. Are you a friend or an enemy, Luke?"

"I'm just the fiancé of the maid of honor."

"Mmm. Okay. I heard that you two were supposed to get married tomorrow, until you had the blowout tonight. Nice fight, by the way. If you weren't acting, then I know how you feel."

Luke drew in a breath.

"But let's say that you were acting. I'd guess that if you were acting, then your lady friend—I sincerely hope you didn't pick her up on the sidewalk—probably doesn't want to marry you. So let's find out."

Too late Luke heard movement behind him. He turned and a hand throttled him, cutting off the air in his throat. The cold nose of a gun barrel pressed to his chin. He recognized the muscle from the boat.

"If your fiancée shows up tomorrow, hoping to marry her beloved, then you live. If not, then, well, I haven't gone shark fishing for a while."

"We broke up. She's probably packing for the mainland right now."

"Maybe. But Lucia is delivering her best friend a letter. From you. Apologizing. Begging for a second chance. You do believe in second chances, don't you, Luke?"

Uh, actually, well, no. But he wanted to. Oh, he wanted to. Preferably, however, with Scarlett safely off this island, back in Rochester. Then he'd track her down, his hat in his hand, so to speak.

He'd apologize. Beg for a second chance. Hope that she believed him.

But not yet.

"She's my fiancée, and she knows my handwriting. She's going to know it's not from me."

"Then let's hope she thinks you wrote it in the throes of emotion and believes it to be your desperate attempt to win back her heart."

Desperate, yes, but desperate to keep her out of danger.

This wouldn't turn out well. If she showed up, she'd jeopardize Lucia's safety. If she didn't, then Claudio would suspect the truth, and at the very least, they'd lose Augusto.

And Luke would find himself dragging behind Claudio's yacht.

He didn't want to guess what Claudio might do to Scarlett.

Please, God, don't let Scarlett show up tomorrow.

But he got it then. Claudio's plan was suddenly painfully clear. Augusto wouldn't show until Scarlett showed up.

THIRTEEN

"Is this for real?"

Scarlett sat on her double bed, the lights of the town below, the air conditioner blasting canned air.

She longed to be outside, to let the salty air clear her head. She'd changed into her capris and a sleeveless shirt, intending on doing just that when Lucia knocked on her door.

"It's from Luke," she said, pressing a letter into Scarlett's hands.

Scarlett let her in without a comment.

"He left it for me in my stateroom, with a note to deliver it to you." Lucia pulled up a chair, her face drawn.

Dear Scarlett,
I was wrong to accuse you, I know that. Please take me back. Please marry me tomorrow. I will wait for you at the altar.
Love, Luke

Love, Luke? What on earth? She looked up and read the question in Lucia's eyes. "He wants me back.

Has asked me to meet him at the altar." She shook her head.

"Really?"

No. Because without a sliver of doubt she knew Luke would have never sent this letter. Even if she longed to believe it.

I was wrong. Oh, sure, she could imagine him writing those words. *Please marry me tomorrow.* Uh-huh.

Please don't let him have had a gun to his head while he wrote that. The thought turned her body to ice.

Lucia got up, sitting beside her on the bed. "I'm so sorry about your terrible fight. Maybe he's trying to make up."

"You know it's just for show, right? We didn't really fight because we aren't really engaged. We don't really love each other."

Lucia said nothing, her dark eyes on her, and Scarlett got up, walking away from her stare.

Yes, Lucia could probably see the truth. But it didn't matter.

"Luke didn't send this. I know it. Not after we disentangled ourselves from the entire mess and left him on duty to protect you. No, he wouldn't drag me back in."

"Then who did?"

She stared at the letter, at the tight, messy handwriting. She didn't know Luke's, but she imagined that his would be neat and crisp.

"I don't know. Maybe the person who is trying to hurt you. Maybe they figured out that we aren't really a couple."

"You look like a couple. Especially tonight on the dance floor."

"When we had our spectacular fight? Oh, yes, he certainly didn't pull any punches—"

"No, when you were dancing. You had your eyes closed and you looked…happy. You looked as if you belonged in each other's arms."

Scarlett shook her head. "I think this fairy tale has played out long enough. We don't belong together, even if I'd like to think so. He's some sort of secret agent, and I'm just a temp. It would never work."

Even if she longed to believe what she'd seen in his eyes.

Lucia opened her mouth, as if to speak, and Scarlett held up a finger to stop her.

"No. What matters is that someone else, not Luke, sent this note. Which means that…"

"Luke is in trouble."

Lucia said the words in a whisper that made Scarlett sink back onto the bed. Luke, in trouble. She should have expected that, but the words grabbed her breath.

"Did you knock at his stateroom door?"

"Yes, but he wasn't there."

"Did you check his villa?"

"I came right here."

Scarlett folded up the letter, stood and shoved it into her pocket. "C'mon."

Luke's villa remained dark after she'd pounded on the door. She glanced at Lucia, then made an executive decision. "We're going in the back."

Cutting between the villas, she ditched her flip-flops and ventured out onto the rocky shore that edged the cottages. The sea sprinkled cold breath upon her skin. She smelled a storm in the air.

"I think this is a terrible idea," Lucia said, holding on to the railing that edged his deck. "He's probably asleep."

"Then he's fine, and I can ask him why he sent me this weird note."

"True love."

"Stop that. He's not in love with me. Be careful." She picked her way along the coral, wincing as it cut into her toes. The terrain dipped into craggy holes, crannies of briny water. Her shirt stuck to her body, seawater dripping down her back. Gooseflesh raised at the raw lick of the wind.

"I'm going to get Benito," Lucia said, hanging on to the edge of the balcony.

"Have you lost your mind? Just go back to the front door. I'll go through and let you in."

"You're the one who's lost her mind." But Lucia crept back to safety as Scarlett stood on the edge of the balcony rail, then reached up and gripped the lower edge of Luke's balcony. She hoisted herself up.

The last time she'd done pull-ups had been in eleventh grade, for her health class graduation requirements. Now, she held herself long enough to hook her toe, then her foot on the edge, working herself onto the ledge.

A very thin ledge. But enough to grip the top of the railing and pull herself to a standing position. Then she threw her leg over the top and tumbled over.

Her shirt caught, ripping as she fell. She bumped a metal chair with her chin, the pain making her see gray dots as she hit the cement. Her foot caught a pot of geraniums. The flowers crashed to the cement, the sound harsh in the night. She stilled, listening.

Nothing except the roar of the waves, the thunder of her own heartbeat.

And, if Luke had been sleeping, he'd already be out here in his skivvies.

The sliding door opened easily, and that, too, had her stomach clenching.

She entered, clinging to the slim hope—and yes, praying—that he might be asleep in his bed.

No. The room remained empty, and just in case he might be hurt, on the floor in a pool of blood—thank you, romantic-suspense-novel imagination—she flicked on the light.

Nothing. No Luke, sleeping like a baby in the middle of his king-size bed. In fact, the bedsheets weren't even mussed.

And, because her overactive imagination still saw a scuffle here, saw Luke being outmanned and wrestled into submission, she checked for evidence. Nothing on the side tables, the floor…

Except there, under the desk, lay his cell phone. Strange place for a cell phone.

She picked it up. *Luke, where are you?*

A knock at the door reminded her that Lucia waited outside. She opened it.

Lucia snuck in, her head ducked. "I don't like this."

Scarlett closed the door behind her. "He's not here."

"Told you. He's probably at the cabana."

"What, drinking his sorrows away? Luke doesn't drink, remember?" She opened the phone. The last number dialed had been an international number.

Lucia began to nose around the room. "A broken heart can make a man betray himself."

"Luke doesn't have a broken heart. Look around, see if you can find—"

"Oh, no."

Scarlett turned. Lucia held what looked like a cigarette butt between her fingers. "This is bad. This brand is from Panama. Benito's father smokes them."

Benito's father?

"I think Claudio was here."

Claudio. The man who'd suspected them on the yacht, who'd made them kiss, who—

"This note is from Claudio." Scarlett said it more as a fact than a question.

"Yes. He must think you and Luke are lying." Lucia sank onto the bed. "I wonder if he thinks I am lying."

"Don't jump to conclusions." Scarlett sat next to Lucia. "You've come this far. Don't give up. We're so close."

"This is such a bad idea. I should just tell Benito the truth, make him elope with me. Who cares about—"

"Your murdered best friend? Justice? The thousands of other victims of the Sanchez drug and trafficking operation?"

Lucia drew in a breath and whisked the moisture from under her eyes. Her hands trembled. "Okay. Yes. But why would Claudio want you to come to the wedding?"

"Maybe to test me? An agent would follow orders, right? If Luke told me to stay away, a good agent would stick to the plan. Because if she didn't, people would get hurt."

"Right. And a true love would meet her man at the altar."

"It's a test to see if it's safe." She drew in a breath. Of course. She looked at the phone. "If I show up, then all is well, and Augusto shows up, too. If I don't, then he's a no-show."

"And all this is in vain."

"Right. I need to show up for Augusto to arrive. But

if I show up, then Luke has to protect both of us. One of us could get hurt. The mission could be in jeopardy. And Augusto could get away."

She let the words die as the scent of the oncoming storm filled the room.

Finally, Lucia asked, "What are you going to do?"

She stared at the phone. "I don't know." She looked at herself in the mirror.

Her hair had fallen from her ponytail, her chin was scraped where she'd hit the chair, her shirt torn from the balcony railing. A raccoon sunburn covered her face, the tops of her shoulders. She appeared a mess, at best. At worst, a liability.

"I am the wrong person for this job. I don't know what I was thinking. That I was some sort of superheroine or something? I've read one too many novels."

Lucia met her gaze in the mirror. The woman always seemed so beautiful, so poised. Now, she, too, appeared bedraggled, her hair in snarls, her eyes reddened. She took Scarlett's hand. "When Juliet showed up murdered, I was so angry. I hatched a plan to bring the Sanchez family to justice. But I was just a law student at Columbia—what was I going to do? I knew Spanish, and I knew my way around the elite society of Panama, thanks to my father's job, so I just ignored the voices in my head and flung myself into fate, praying it wouldn't betray me."

She sighed. "I've done a lot of things because of this crusade that I regret. Starting with tricking Benito, to leaving a trail of lies until I found myself ready to betray him. I am a Judas, and I thought for sure I was lost, forgotten—and then you and Luke showed up. You have been a better friend to me than I deserve. And now, even though it will cost me Benito, Juliet's murderer will be brought to justice. Not only that, but a major cartel will be taken down."

"Oh, Lucia, I am nothing like you. You're beautiful and smart and brave. I'm just a girl who got in the wrong cab and found herself in over her head."

"My mother used to say that we don't know who we are until we are pushed beyond ourselves. You are more than you think. You're the heroine who stepped in to keep me sane during the last few days. You're the one who didn't let me down. You're exactly who I needed. And now you're going to be who Luke needs, too."

"Who is that?"

Lucia looked at the cell phone. "Let's find out."

Even God had conspired against him. The storm over the sea last night, resulting in a change of wedding venue and thus destroying the Stryker team's plans could only be considered divine payback.

And why not? Luke had made nothing but mistakes since he'd arrived in Mexico, flying by the seat of his pants—again, on instincts.

Pretty much the way he'd always gotten himself into trouble.

Like when he'd punched out his commanding officer and been neatly discharged from his career as navy SEAL.

Or when he'd let his emptiness deliver him into the arms of a married woman.

And when he'd hijacked Scarlett from her safe life into his crazy, dangerous world and let his heart find healing in her smile.

Yes, that might be the worst part of this entire debacle, the fact that he'd let himself feel again. Let himself wonder what it might be like to trust someone with his heart again.

Please, Scarlett, be on a plane over the ocean right now.

But probably, her flight had been grounded, just another check mark on the list of things that could go wrong on this mission.

And, as if God had a sense of humor, Luke would die dressed like a cruise lounge singer.

Luke stood next to Benito, smiling for fifty of their closest underworld friends, gun sights traced to his head. Beyond the cabana, the debris from last night's storm littered the shore. Luke's stomach still roiled. Years in the military had turned his stomach to steel, but now his nausea had little to do with seasickness. Locking him in his stateroom bathroom might have been a good idea after all.

Claudio had at least let him clean up for his big day, although Luke's bright idea to turn his disposable razor into a sort of weapon died under the scrutiny of his guards, whom he'd decided to call Juan and Paulo.

Juan didn't go down easily, as Luke discovered as they'd wrestled him onto the boat, and Paulo had a killer right hook. The way he looked, the wedding guests might actually think Luke had tracked down Duncan and gone a couple of rounds.

Winner gets the girl.

Luke had lost, though he now stood at the altar with the other groom. Looking resplendent in his white suit, despite his licks, as if he'd won back the bride. He was probably the only groom in history, however, who prayed his bride wouldn't show.

Because that would only add another layer of disaster to this day's events.

He hadn't seen Lucia or Scarlett yet, but that hardly mattered, because Chet and his merry band of commandos were probably scaling the cliffs at the other end of the resort, unaware that Lucia and Benito wouldn't be tying the knot under the pavilion, but in the cabana next to the beach. Where the clear view of the sea prevented any stealth attack.

Perfect.

And had Luke been able to alert Chet? Not unless the man had developed telepathic abilities.

No, this entire mission was about to go into the drink, and Lucia would end up married to Benito, and then what? Betrayal would get extra messy.

"Are you sure Scarlett's going to change her mind?" Benito said. Not a little surprise had crossed his face when Luke arrived, gun pressed to his back, dressed for matrimony. Which gave Luke a small rise of hope that the man hadn't been involved in Lucia's death attempts after all. Maybe he did love her.

Criminals fell in love, too, right? After all, look at Luke.

No. He couldn't let himself love Scarlett. Couldn't love the way she smiled at him, the way she looked at him as if he might be some sort of action hero. Couldn't love the trust in her eyes, the way she kissed him—

Oh, boy. He managed a smile for Benito. "I hope so."

Benito gave him a wink as the music started.

Luke scanned the crowd. The guests sat in chairs, draped white for the event, two rows with a center aisle. A blood-red carpet led up to the floral arch under which the priest waited. Two Lost Breezes staff members stood outside the cabana, ushering the noninvited guests to other parts of the resort. In the corner, the bartender tried to look unobtrusive, restocking the bar. A white-gloved usher stood with his back turned, as if waiting for the bride.

Not brides. Please, not brides, plural. Because, really, why would Scarlett risk her life again for him? After the way he'd treated her? After the things he'd said that reopened her wounds?

No, she wouldn't—shouldn't—show up. Because he didn't deserve her.

He glanced at Claudio sitting in the front row, smiling as guests congratulated him.

Would they shoot him right off, or would they wait until the end of the ceremony? Probably it would be something private, and as Claudio said, it would involve sharks.

As for Augusto, well, Luke had pegged that right. So far, no Scarlett, thus, no Augusto.

If Luke had been working with Stacey, he would have expected her to show. Expected her even to know how to line up help protecting Lucia. But Scarlett—

I'm sorry, God. I let You down. I let us all down.

The music started. A flautist stepped up and, accompanied by the keyboardist, began an aria that, had it been his own wedding, might have made him start to tremble.

He, like Benito, turned to look at the end of the aisle, to admire the bride as she stepped up to—

Scarlett was lined up right behind Lucia, and while Lucia appeared a radiant beauty, Scarlett could stop his heart in his chest.

And right then, he actually wanted it to be true. Wanted to be standing at the altar, a groom waiting for his bride. This bride.

Scarlett had swept up her hair, ringlets hanging down

to frame her face. A splash of sunshine warmed her nose. He couldn't meet her eyes. He didn't want to see the hope in them.

He didn't want her to see his fear.

No, God, this wasn't—

Luke had made his peace with God, sitting in that bathroom all night. Made peace with the fact that he'd screwed up, and that while he'd slink into heaven, perhaps, it would only be out of a divine contract of redemption, not because God actually wanted him there. Still, he was ready to face up to his betrayals, to his mistakes.

He was ready to die.

But Scarlett was not.

"Oh, no."

Benito looked at him and he realized he'd spoken out loud. He flashed Benito a quick, hard smile.

"Getting cold feet?"

Freezing. But then, he let himself look at Scarlett, finally meet her eyes.

Instead of a bright, love-struck shine, he read calm. She didn't even flinch as she looked at him, confidence on her face, as if she might be saying "Trust me."

Trust me.

Oh, God, he wanted to. And even as he thought it, he realized that yes, yes, he did trust her. Did believe in her.

Trust me.

Except, now he heard a whisper inside, something other than his own voice. *Trust Me.*

Yes.

Please, yes. I want to trust You, God.

Because, despite his betrayals, despite his mistakes,

God had sent him Scarlett. To heal his heart. To show him that no, not all women lie.

Some of them, in fact, surprise you with their loyalty.

And that's when a man appeared behind Lucia. Six feet of nasty slicked up for the day. He edged up behind her, grinning to his nephew as he slipped past both brides and into the cabana.

And Lucia met his eyes and nodded.

Augusto.

Leaner than Claudio, Augusto bore the Sanchezes' dark looks, although a scar ran along his cheekbone, as if he, too, understood betrayal. From the front row, Claudio stood, and for a moment, the crowd watched what might have been, in a different time and place, with a different family, a heartwarming embrace.

Two brothers, reunited.

Two murderers, sharing a moment.

Yes, Luke might be ill again, right on Benito's shiny white shoes.

Then, chaos erupted.

The flautist dropped to her knees, abandoning her instrument and pulling from her case a handgun while the bartender turned and—hello, *Chet!*—produced a Glock he'd clearly smuggled in with the rum.

"Freeze, Augusto!" called one of the resort staff who suddenly appeared armed and advancing on Augusto. Vicktor Shubuikov, Stryker operative who'd shed his Russian accent and added a tan.

Then he spotted his pal Brody, who had—thank You God—moved in front of Lucia, as if that's what all resort employees did when weapons appeared.

Every man in the wedding party, save Luke, produced

weapons, including Claudio, who backed up in front of his brother. "Stay back!"

Claudio directed his words at the cadre of vested CIA agents who surrounded the cabana, their semiautomatic weapons trained at the guests, most of whom hit the sandy floor, their heads covered.

It happened so fast that Luke barely processed the entire scenario. His eyes found Scarlett.

Still that calm, almost confident gaze.

And then, someone fired.

He saw her flinch, and that's what made him launch himself toward her, although he might have already been moving. More shots, more screaming.

Scarlett.

Luke had one thought, even as he saw Benito fall, even as the man started to writhe, hands pressed to his gut, blood spurting between his fingers.

"Help!" Benito cried.

Luke glanced at him and in that blink of time, Scarlett vanished. He turned back to the groom, who looked up with pain in his eyes. "What's going on? Where is Lucia?"

Seriously? Could it be that Benito really hadn't put the pieces together?

"I'll find her," Luke said, and he meant it. Because, indeed, even a criminal could fall in love. He pulled off his jacket, wadded it up and shoved it against Benito's abdomen. "Hold on."

Then, he dove toward the flautist. She'd taken a position behind the piano, holding her own as a bullet pinged past her.

"Stacey," she said fast, not sparing Luke a glance. "Sorry I'm late."

"I need a weapon," he said. She nodded toward one

of Claudio's men, bleeding out not a few feet away. "Where's Augusto?"

"I don't know. Somewhere in the mass of people."

Talk about a mess. Still, maybe some semblance of the plan remained intact. Get Lucia. Put her on the chopper. He left Stacey—who, yes, would have made a good stand-in as maid of honor with her ability to shoot straight—and took off, scrambling over the walled edge of the cabana, scooting around to the entrance.

No Lucia.

And no Scarlett, who he hoped had run screaming from the shooting. Not a chance, probably.

He crouched next to the entrance, praying Brody had grabbed them both.

"Luke! Over here!" Brody gestured from the door of a scuba hut.

Luke scrabbled across the sand, and hallelujah, he nearly broke out into tears when he spotted Scarlett with her arms clasped around a sobbing Lucia.

So much for the perfect wedding day.

But when Scarlett looked up at him, tears smearing her makeup, surrounded by the ruffles of her beautiful dress, he wanted to cry a little, too.

"Are you okay?"

She nodded.

Thank You, thank You, God.

He turned to Brody. "Chopper waiting?"

"Yep." And then Brody gave him a wink. "Fancy duds."

"Just cover us."

He took one look at Lucia and scooped her up in his arms. "On my tail, Scarlett. Don't look back."

Then, with Lucia's face buried in his chest, his bride

hanging on to his pocket, Luke swept out of the scuba hut and across the damp sand toward the chopper.

Shouts and gunshots pinged around him, and he knew someone had seen him escaping with the brides. "Run, Scarlett!"

He ran off the path, putting the playground, the hammocks, the snack hut between them and the shooters until finally he spotted their getaway vehicle, a majestic Seahawk.

His cohort at Stryker International, Mae Lund-Stryker, sat at the controls, gesturing them on board the special-ops chopper, her red hair in a braid down her back.

Luke set Lucia on the deck. "Nice ride. You borrow this from the navy?"

Mae grinned at him. "Something like that. Let's go!"

Luke turned, intending to hoist Scarlett on board. "C'mon, Scarlett!"

But she stood away from him, a look on her face that stopped his blood cold.

In fact, his world ground to a halt with one quiet word.

"No."

FOURTEEN

"No?"

Luke stared at her, actually repeating her word. *"No?"*

And for a second, Scarlett's resolve wavered. She returned in her mind to that moment at the door of the cabana, the sky clearing behind her, the red carpet before her, her groom waiting at the altar, when she'd wished, with everything inside her, that this might be real.

That she might be the bride, with this breathtakingly handsome groom waiting for her, an unexpected life ahead. Something permanent.

No longer a temp.

Because, as she'd stood there, she'd known, as if some sort of voice from heaven had spoken, that only Luke could be her hero. Only in his arms could she find her happily ever after. And, while he thought they were still on a mission, she'd stopped playing games.

Probably that first time he kissed her.

She wanted to kiss him now. Wanted to throw herself into his arms, to fling herself back into the fairy tale.

To be the princess.

But the gunshots in the distance, the shouting, cut

into her dream and shook her back to reality. "No." She gathered up her dress and took another step back. "This is where it ends."

"What are you talking about? Get on the chopper, Scarlett. We don't have any time—"

"*You* don't have any time. I have one more day of vacation and a wedding to get to."

He frowned at her, confusion on his face.

"My sister is getting married today, remember? In about an hour."

"And—?" Luke stared at her. "She doesn't want you there."

She tried not to flinch at that. "I know, but it doesn't matter."

"Scarlett—"

"Luke, I stood there, ready to walk down the aisle to you, and I saw your fear. I wanted the happily ever after for us, but it isn't real. I know you were afraid of your mission going south—"

"Of you getting killed!"

"But Bridgett wore that same look when I accused her of stealing Duncan at the engagement party. She was truly afraid I'd take him away. She loves him, Luke. And even if I am not in the wedding, she deserves my blessing."

Even as she said it, the truth burrowed inside. Despite Bridgett's narrow world, Scarlett had made it smaller with her hurt, her wounded attitude. Instead of joining in on the joy, as Lucia had done yesterday for her make-believe wedding, Scarlett had begrudged Bridgett happiness.

Sure, she'd filled in. But she'd never really been part of the fun, a part of the joy.

And perhaps that's why Bridgett had turned on the nasty.

No more. At least one sister would get her fairytale wedding, her happily ever after today.

"I have to go to my sister's wedding," she said again, this time with finality in her voice.

Again, a confused look from Luke. "I don't understand. After everything she's done—"

"Luke, that's why I'm here." She continued to back away, now gathering up the tremendous layers of silk. She would keep the dress. Maybe ship it home.

And what? Wear it around the house on Saturday mornings? Remember how Luke appeared when he burst into the scuba house, panic on his face? How his gaze had landed on Lucia with such relief?

How she'd wished that he'd been running after her?

That was the problem, wasn't it? He'd been here to protect *Lucia*. Not to sweep Scarlett off her feet. He proved that when he picked up Lucia and ran with her to the chopper. *On my tail, Scarlett!* She was always just the afterthought.

"Go, Luke. I'm fine. The cavalry is here and I have a taxi waiting. Go with Lucia." She steadied her voice, kept it firm.

But he didn't move. "Did you—did you arrange this?"

"I called your pal Chet last night. He and I figured out some communication. I didn't think I'd be able to go through with it until I saw the bartender wink at me. I guessed it might be your friend. I knew then that we'd be in good hands."

"So you put this together." Luke shook his head as if still trying to comprehend her words.

"No, you did. I just helped you finish it."

"Scarlett, I don't know how to thank—"

"You don't have to. But this is goodbye, Luke."

"Luke! Chet just radioed in. They caught Augusto. It's over. Get in—the team is on their way," the pilot called.

Scarlett saw the debate in his eyes. He glanced back at Lucia, who had curled into a ball, sobbing.

She took the opportunity to turn away before he saw her tears, before she got onto that chopper and only prolonged the pain. Because then what? They'd get back to the mainland, get Lucia calmed down and then Luke would turn to her and…declare his undying love? Propose?

The story just didn't end that way for girls like Scarlett. Especially not with heroes like Luke. She'd never been the pretty one, the one the boys wanted. And as soon as the game was over, Luke would snap out of whatever feelings he'd conjured for her in order to complete his mission, thank her—as he was about to do now—and give her a one-way ticket back to Rochester.

She had to walk out of the story first, if only to give herself a moment of dignity.

"Scarlett!" She heard his voice at her back, but the chopper churned up his words. She cast a look over her shoulder as Luke's team ran up to the chopper—the bartender, the flautist and the valet who'd whipped out some sort of weaponry and thrown her and Lucia to the ground before ushering them to the scuba hut.

Clearly, not an employee of the Lost Breezes Hotel.

"C'mon, Luke!" the man yelled, and Scarlett took that as her cue.

She hit the sidewalk, scampered up the stairs to her hotel and opened the door to the lobby.

She didn't look back as she heard the chopper roar, preparing to lift off into the sky.

The hushed coolness of the hotel with its piped-in music belied the rush of her heartbeat. She spied Raoul standing by the door, white-gloved, glancing past her to the chopper, his face knotted in confusion.

"Taxi?"

"Uh…as you wish, *señorita*." He opened the door and whistled. One of the hotel town cars pulled up. He held the door for her as she passed. "I thought your sister was the one getting married. Are you getting married today, too?" Raoul glanced at her dress.

Scarlett shook her head. "He…backed out."

"I'm so sorry." He opened the car door for her.

"It's okay. I expected it."

"His loss." Yes, well. His relief, more likely.

She leaned back in to the seat, closing her eyes. "The lighthouse, please."

The car started forward, then jerked to a stop. She opened her eyes and caught herself on the seat in front of her as she flew forward. A body stood in front of the car, then circled to the passenger side.

Beside her, the door opened. "Leaving already?" Claudio said as he slid in beside her. He draped his arm over the back of her seat, then pressed his gun to the driver's neck. "Drive."

"Where are we going?" She couldn't believe words actually came out of her mouth, but they did, and they sounded angry. Huh. Good for her.

"On a little boat ride."

And then she had no words at all.

"Benito!"

Luke tore himself away from the view of Scarlett

running away from him and looked toward the voice behind him, screaming. Lucia was nearly crazy with horror as Chet and Brody carried Benito to the chopper, Benito with one arm over each of their shoulders. Vicktor, their Russian compatriot who'd played the role of white-gloved usher, clasped Benito's legs.

They settled him on the deck as Lucia grabbed his hands. "Benito, oh, I'm sorry, I'm sorry!"

Luke came at them, his training kicking in. Brody was already at work over Benito as Luke removed his jacket from Benito's grip, now sodden with blood. He looked at the wound. Two more inches and the bullet would have hit him instead. "Help me search for an exit wound, guys."

Brody moved to his side as Benito groaned.

"Got one."

Good. One bullet, two holes. The math added up. And it didn't look too serious, out of reach of major organs. "It's a clean through-and-through it seems. But he needs a hospital."

Lucia scooted Benito's head onto her lap. "Oh, I'm sorry. I didn't want you to get hurt."

"I know," he said softly. His eyes held tenderness. "I know."

Luke stared at him, trying to sort out his reaction. Lucia, too, because she looked up at Luke. Benito took her hand. "I knew about the information you were leaking to the CIA." He glanced at Luke. "You were sent here to protect her, right?"

Luke nodded.

"I thought so. Well, at first. And then I wasn't so sure. I thought you really loved Scarlett."

I did. The words nearly made it out but Chet peered at

him with a frown. Brody was breaking out the medical kit.

I do. That's what he meant to say.

What he'd wanted to say.

Would have said, if she'd made it all the way up to the altar, if they had gone through with the wedding. I do. And I do again, later, after she had a chance to figure out what she wanted. If she wanted him.

Which, she clearly didn't.

No. This is goodbye, Luke. That was a clear message. At least she hadn't lied to him, told him she loved him.

He must have dreamed up that part from his wishful, broken heart.

He looked again at Benito. "You knew about Lucia?"

Brody handed Luke a syringe of morphine. He injected it into Benito's leg.

"Yeah," he rasped. "And I knew that someone was trying to hurt her. I thought it might be one of my father's valets, but then I began to think it might be my father. Especially after everyone on the boat—including you and Scarlett—came back clean."

"You knew about the raid?" Lucia said.

He closed his eyes and nodded. Luke snapped on a pair of gloves.

"Are we all in?" Mae asked.

"Just about. Give me a second here," Luke said as he wrapped Benito's arm in a rubber tube, searching for a vein. "Wait until I get this IV in."

"I knew. But I also knew why. I'm so sorry about your friend, Lucia. I figured out why you were here a long time ago. But I didn't care. I loved you, Lucia, and I hoped I could earn your love. Your trust. It's not all that easy to leave the family, and I hoped…"

He winced as Luke started an IV. Clearly the narcotics hadn't entered his system yet.

"...I hoped that when the time came, you'd tell me." He lifted her hand and kissed it. "I was hoping we could start over, a new life in America. Or...anywhere."

Benito glanced at Luke, who looked at Chet. He nodded. Probably, yes, they could work that out. Benito's testimony, on top of catching Augusto, would seal the deal on the demise of the Sanchez operation.

"I forgive you, Lucia. I don't care that you betrayed me. I know you love me. And I want to start over."

Start over.

But that was just it, wasn't it? How could they start over with so much against them? With their mistakes and sins and betrayals?

"Marry me today," Benito said. "At the hospital. Please?"

Her expression made Luke turn away. See, that was what he wanted.

The chopper lurched, and Luke lost his balance, nearly tumbling out. "Wait!" Chet yelled, turned to Luke. "Where's Scarlett?"

"She left," Luke said. He couldn't manage more than that, but Benito gave him a look that might have been followed with a good shaking if he'd been able to move.

"She left?"

Luke looked away and checked the man's pulse.

"Did you tell her that you love her?"

And then he couldn't answer because shame welled up inside his throat, choking him. After all she'd done, after she'd saved all their lives... "It's better this way."

"For who?" Benito thundered, which did nothing for his pulse.

It didn't matter, however, because Chet was pulling Luke out of the chopper, to Mae's shrieks of fury. He separated Luke from the whir of the chopper, Luke's shirt in his fist. "What's going on?"

"I…"

"Are you in love with this woman?"

And Luke looked up into the eyes of the man who had taught him what it meant to take a risk on love, to heal and move forward, despite the horrors of the past, and he could do nothing but nod.

"Then why are you still standing here?"

"Because…because what if I turn out like my old man?"

And there it lay, raw and horrid, and Chet looked at him and…smirked?

"You are so not your old man, Luke. You aren't even close."

"What about D.C.?"

"What about D.C.? That happened two years ago. This is about now. And you being a very different guy. A changed guy. A guy who's staring a second chance in the face."

A second chance.

"Don't live your life looking over your shoulder at the guy you were, Luke. Run after the guy you know you can be. The guy God will help you be. 'Forgetting what is behind and focusing on what lies ahead, run the race set before you…' We all make mistakes, Luke. But that's what grace and new mercies every morning are about. Trusting God to wipe the slate clean and give us a second chance."

Looking forward, not behind. Choosing to trust, not to fear.

Choosing loyalty, not betrayal.

Because even though he'd been unfaithful to God, God hadn't, *couldn't* be unfaithful to him. Because God wasn't a betrayer. He was truth and honesty and loyalty and love.

And Luke had a glimpse of what that looked like, felt like, in Scarlett.

Maybe getting into her cab had been the second chance he'd been longing for. Who knew her undercover identity had been that of Happily-Ever-After Girl?

And he'd let her go.

"Besides," Chet said, "we don't have room in the chopper. You'll have to find your own ride back to the mainland." Chet reached into his pocket and pressed his cell phone into Luke's hand. "And don't leave us hanging." Then he turned and ran back to the chopper.

Mae lifted off into the blue sky.

Luke turned and ran toward the hotel.

Please, please let him not be too late. He looked a mess—dirty and covered in blood, his white pants showing the day's chaos. He sprinted up to the hotel and around the outside, hoping to catch her at the taxi stand.

Raoul stood, staring out after a town car as it motored down the road, over the bridge, toward the city center.

"Raoul! Was Scarlett here?"

Raoul seemed to look right through Luke. "He got in with her."

"Who got in with her? What are you talking about?"

"Mr. Sanchez. He got into the car with Scarlett. And he had a gun."

Mr. Sanchez. Claudio. "Was it Benito's father? Big guy, older than the groom?"

Raoul nodded.

No, no, no. Luke sprinted toward one of the rental

scooters, lifting it off its kickstand. "Run to the cabana and tell the CIA that Claudio has Scarlett."

The scooter nearly wheelied out of the lot as he full-throttled it over the bridge after the town car.

Claudio wasn't going anywhere with Luke's girl.

"Get out of my cab!"

Claudio actually laughed. He put his gun in her face and laughed.

Scarlett had never truly understood the expression "a cold streak of fear" until that moment.

"You fooled me with your little game. I thought you were the real thing," Claudio said, pointing his gun again at the cabbie, who had shrunken down as low as he could go.

"Drive us to the marina at the far end of the island." Claudio turned to Scarlett. "I sent my yacht to anchor offshore this morning, after we disembarked. It seemed wise, just in case…" He smiled at her, baring his teeth.

"Please, Claudio, it's over. They just wanted your brother."

"You have destroyed my life! My son, betrayed. My family broken!" He poured his fury out, and she thought she might throw up.

Okay, yes, now she understood Luke's fear for her. Now it felt real, ugly. Deadly.

"I should have listened to my instincts. I knew Lucia was lying. I knew you were lying."

"You're the one who was trying to kill her."

"Scare her. Enough for the truth to come out. For her to run. Clearly it was not enough."

He clamped his hand around her upper arm. "But now

she'll see that she should keep her mouth shut. She'll see what happens to people who betray the family."

Scarlett clasped her hands together to keep them from shaking. *Please, God. Please. I'm sorry I didn't see You waving me off sooner.* Why had she treated this as a game? Why had she gotten herself in over her head?

She should have shown up, given her sister an amazing wedding and returned home to her paperbacks. Maybe adopted a cat. Why had she thought she could be some sort of hero?

A thump rocked the car and the cabbie nearly swerved off into a white-painted palm tree. Then she saw legs kicking at the back window and a hand slamming the passenger door and—

Luke! Like some sort of superhero he had landed on top of the car!

She lunged for the door but Claudio grabbed her arm and rolled down his window. He leaned out, aiming the gun at the roof.

"Luke, look out!" She launched herself at Claudio, clawing at his arm. He squeezed off two shots, but they went wild into the air.

The cabbie was shouting. Claudio slammed his hand into her jaw.

Pain exploded in her eyes and she fell back. Then, hallelujah, she hit the door. Blinking back dots and praying she wouldn't be trapped in the tulle, she lunged for the door handle.

The door popped open just as Claudio swore. She turned back to see her shoe connect with his face.

Oh, God, please help me.

She stared at the pavement streaking by, then with every ounce of courage she had, she launched herself from the door to freedom.

Yes, she'd seen it done in movies but this was very different. The ground had never felt quite so hard, the pavement so hot, and she yowled as she tried to land on her feet. She tripped and skidded into the curb, banging into a row of motor scooters.

One crashed down on top of her, pinning her.

Then she lay there, because her entire body felt as if it had turned to fire.

"Scarlett!"

She heard him beyond the rubble, heard his grunts as he fought with the bikes. "Are you okay? Please be okay!"

She wanted to say yes, but she hadn't yet found her voice.

Then, suddenly, she was free. And scooped up.

Her heart stopped right there. She hadn't left the fairy tale behind at all. Here he was, her prince, staring at her as if he'd nearly lost her forever.

"Are you okay?" he asked again.

She thought so. She managed a nod as he pressed his forehead to hers and she felt his entire body tremble.

Then, the screech of brakes, and shouting. Luke looked up, searching for the noise. He didn't have to tell her. She could read his face.

The car had slammed into a whitened palm tree. But Claudio had kicked open the door. He rounded and saw them.

He raised his gun.

"Can you ride?" Luke set her down.

She scooped up her dress.

He grabbed her hand and began to run back down the street where his scooter lay on its side. A shot fired. Then another. She stifled a scream. Luke looked back.

Please, God, let the driver be okay. Don't let anyone get shot!

Luke let go of her hand, reached the bike and pulled it upright. "Get on!"

He didn't have to tell her twice. She tossed the train of her dress over her arm and jumped on behind him, barely catching his waist as the bike tore away.

"Where are the good guys?" she yelled into his ear.

"It's just us, honey. Hold on." They shot past scooters, cars, pedestrians.

Just us.

How she liked the sound of that.

Behind them, she heard an engine and turned.

Claudio had found new wheels and was burning up the pavement toward them.

Oh, she took it back. She might have liked company, namely that shiny black chopper, to swoop from the sky.

"Hang on!" Luke shouted as he left the pavement, bumping over the curb to the boardwalk.

Claudio's "borrowed" car flew over the embankment, scattering people and pigeons. Scarlett tightened her grip around Luke's waist as she glanced back.

Just in time to see Claudio stick his arm out the window, gun in hand.

She screamed as he began to shoot.

FIFTEEN

Luke just might get them both killed after all. He had the scooter throttle wide open, topping out at a mind-blowing 50 mph, yelling and laying on his horn as he barreled down the sidewalk along the beach. Mothers grabbed at their children, dogs turned to chase them.

Please don't let any of them be killed by Claudio. In his side mirror, he spotted the lunatic bearing down on them in a car.

And please let Brody have understood his panicked, garbled words. He'd pressed speed dial, pretty sure Chet would have one of the five Stryker team members programmed in. He hit the jackpot when Brody answered, screaming above the shrill chopper noise.

He'd screamed back that he needed help, then got disconnected.

Scarlett's hands locked around him, holding on.

Trusting him.

He'd liked how "just us" spilled out of his mouth.

He hoped to use "us" again. And "we." And "Together." And those pronouns that couples used.

"Hurry up, he's gaining on us!"

Not so much *that* usage of *us*.

God, please, if You were serious about trusting

You, give me a sign. Because I want to trust You, I do, but—

And then he heard it. The glorious sound of a Seahawk chopper hovering overhead, rough and full and thunderous.

He veered hard, bumping off the boardwalk, toward the pier that jutted out to the harbor. The ferries had left, the tourists all disembarked.

They needed a clear area for Brody or Chet to take a shot with one of those mounted machine guns and not hit anybody. Please, don't hit anybody. Except, of course, Claudio.

He gunned it toward the pier, toward the clear blue of the sea, and Scarlett made not a peep, just dug her chin into his shoulder and held on.

Please, let this work. He glanced in the mirror. Claudio took the bait, bearing down on them. He maneuvered them through the gate, but Claudio slammed right through, ten feet away, five, gunning up hard on their tail.

Scarlett's grip on him tightened. Luke swerved the bike back and forth. He needed space between the scooter and Claudio if the Stryker team hoped to open fire. Machine guns weren't known for their accuracy.

Claudio roared up closer.

And in the near distance, he made out the wail of a siren.

Luke had no choice. "Brace yourself, Scarlett! We're going to get wet!"

Just as Claudio caught his bumper, ready to give them a push, Luke cut hard and soared off the edge of the pier, into the clear blue ocean.

As if they could read his mind, Brody and Chet opened up, creating the sound of gunfire in Luke's wake.

He splashed down, still glued to the scooter, Scarlett's arms hooked around his waist. He let the scooter go and kicked up toward the surface.

Scarlett's hands loosened from around him. He turned, reaching for her, but her grip slipped away.

He kicked again, clearing the surface, gulping in air.

"Scarlett!" She hadn't surfaced yet. He turned, searching. "Scarlett!"

He ducked under the water.

There, some fifteen feet down. He saw white as she fought with her dress, caught in the wheels of the scooter.

A fight she was losing, and fast.

He kicked toward her, grabbing the dress. It had spun a couple of times around the wheel, pinning her to the bike. He tugged, but it wouldn't move. His lungs began to burn.

She looked at him, wide-eyed. A bubble emerged from her mouth as her air leaked out. No, no—

Then, he turned her around, grabbed the dress with its thousand tiny buttons and ripped.

It came apart. As her eyes closed, he slipped her arms free, grabbed her around the waist and tugged.

The dress fell away as Luke pulled her free, her white slip like an angelic dress around her. He kicked hard.

By the time he broke the surface, she'd turned gray, her lips cool. "Breathe, Scarlett!"

Breathe. He held her neck with one hand, her nose with the other, and breathed into her mouth while treading water. Her chest rose, fell.

"C'mon, Scarlett!"

Another breath and she spluttered, coughing, her body twisting even as he caught her to himself. "Shh."

He cradled her to his chest as he kicked toward shore, sweeping her into his arms as soon as he hit the beach.

She stared up at him, her eyes wide, still coughing. Shaking, too.

Behind them, Claudio's car sat on the pier, tires blown out, Claudio facedown on the hood of his car, being cuffed by local police.

The chopper blinked out across the horizon. Thank you, Stryker team.

Luke set her down on the sand. His hands trembled and he thought he might throw up. He had to put a hand out, catching himself on the sand before he fell back.

She cleared her throat. "I thought I was going to die."

He didn't mention the fact that she, uh, did.

"Me, too." In fact, the words came out so raw, he cupped his hand over his eyes. And then, he started to cry. Oh, he tried not to. Tried not to turn into an idiot right there on the beach, but —

"It's okay, Luke. I'm okay."

She slipped her hand onto his shoulder. He didn't look at her as he covered her hand with his. He just kept his other hand over his face, trying to rein in his emotions.

"I hope this means you have feelings for me, too."

Oh, Scarlett. He couldn't help the smile. Or the happiness now flooding through him, taking over him. "Yeah. I...have feelings for you."

"Thought so," she said. "And that's convenient, because I need a date to this wedding..."

And then, because she'd washed the fear right out of him, sitting there with the sun at her back in the glow of twilight, he turned to her, cupped his hand to her face and kissed her. A full-on, no-doubt-about-it kiss that she returned with something he'd call gusto. Her arms went around him, and she let him pull her to him. He kissed her as he'd wanted to since she'd gotten into his cab with those ludicrous boots and her winter pallor and turned his world to fire.

Scarlett. She'd made him believe again in second chances, in loyalty, in trust. More than that, in her kiss he tasted his tomorrows, could even see her from the view of the altar, walking down the aisle toward him. He could see himself waking up next to her, to her morning smile. So this was what it felt like to stop living in fear. To trust. To love.

Scarlett. He might have breathed her name, because she pulled back and looked in his eyes. "Hey."

"Hey," he said. "So, uh, see, I, uh…"

"Oh, don't think you're backing out now, double-oh-seven. I blew off two other guys for you. And, frankly, I think you owe me a new dress."

"I think you need a towel. Or a beach wrap." He pulled her close, his arms around her. "Or we could just stay like this."

She wrapped her arms around his waist again. Yes, she could stay like this for as long as she wanted.

"Do you think we could start over, Scarlett? Maybe without the covert undercover stuff?" He hated how much vulnerability he heard in his voice, but well, maybe that was a new Luke, too. One who could show his feelings occasionally.

Sometimes.

"No. I don't think so."

He went still.

She pulled away from him. "Relax, Superman. No, I'm not starting over. I like my new life and I'm keeping it. No more starting over with a new job, a new identity. I'm keeping this one. And I'm keeping you."

She was keeping him.

He kissed her again, softly, like a whisper. "I love you, Scarlett. It scares me to say that, but I can't be an honest man and not tell you that you changed my life."

"No more solo acts?"

"No more solo acts. And I'm not sure how this is going to work, with me traveling so much, but it can, if we want it to. Because I trust you. And I hope you will trust me."

"With my life." She touched her forehead to his. "I love you, too. You make me feel like I'm worth chasing after."

"Oh, you are. I promise, you are." He kissed her cheeks, her forehead, her eyes, and drew back to drink in her smile. "Some wedding, huh?"

She looked at him, her mouth open. "The wedding!"

"Right! The *wedding*." He got up and pulled off his shirt to give her a little extra coverage.

"Should we change first?" she said as she stood, water running down her sand-caked legs, shivering slightly.

He put his arm around her and drew her tight against him. "Naw. You look fabulous just the way you are."

If Scarlett could choose any time, any place to get married, it would be right here, on the south cliffs, under the glow of the lighthouse, with the sun turning to amber on the horizon and streaking the ocean with gold.

It wasn't Scarlett getting married, but that was fine for now, with Luke taking her hand as they ran toward the small ceremony. The floral arch framing the groom,

Duncan resplendent in his tux, the pastor waiting as Bridgett—

Where was Bridgett?

Scarlett saw her standing in the doorway to the lighthouse, hiding.

Bridgett looked up as Scarlett ran up to her, the scared expression upon her face giving over to horror. "Are you okay?"

Scarlett looked herself over. She'd picked up the beach dress with the large red poppies from a vendor and pushed her wet hair into a fake flower at the side of her head. That and a pair of red flip-flops—hey, she wasn't a bridesmaid, right?

"We went swimming," Luke said, looking exactly like a beach bum in his blue floral swimming trunks and white "Surf Mexico" T-shirt. She'd made him take off the Ray-Bans as they got out of the taxi, but other than that, she loved him just the way he was.

He was the real deal. She'd felt it in his kisses, in the way he'd cried after breathing life back into her. No more pretend.

Her sister pursed her lips and Scarlett held up a hand to stave off a meltdown. "I'm sorry we're late. What are you doing here? You should be at the altar, saying 'I do.'"

"Uh, well, I was hoping you'd show up."

Scarlett actually looked behind her. "Me. You were waiting for me?"

Bridgett raised her shoulder and gave her a watery smile.

Uh-oh. All was not well in Bridgett's world. Scarlett glanced at Luke and he stepped to the side but stayed close. "If you think I'm walking away from you after today's events, you've got another thing coming," he said softly.

She smiled at that. Her sister glanced at him, more questions on her face.

"Not now. Tell me why you're really standing here and not at the altar."

Bridgett closed her eyes. "I really was hoping you'd show up. Because…" She opened her teary eyes. "I don't have anyone to give me away."

Oh. Right. Scarlett's voice softened. "Since when did you turn old-fashioned?"

"Since I realized that you're the only family I have left, except for crazy Aunt Gretchen—"

"She's not crazy. Just agoraphobic. And a hoarder. And, well, if you got to know her—"

"Which is the point. I didn't. And I barely know you. I've just been so busy that I missed out. I miss Mom and Dad, and I miss you." She drew in a breath. "I couldn't walk down the aisle without telling you I'm so sorry I fired you."

"Twice."

Her sister's mouth lifted in a smile. "Twice. The wedding is beautiful, Scarlett. I can't believe you did this for me. After all I did to you."

"What did you do to me?" Scarlett asked.

"Oh." She glanced at Luke, who chose now to pull his sunglasses down over his eyes.

Bridgett took a breath. "You were right about my stealing Duncan. I pretty much came back and saw you had the life that I wanted—"

"You wanted to be a temp, with a pile of romance novels for a best friend?"

"Your best friend was Duncan. And you were loyal to him, and I stole him. And now I really do love him, but that doesn't mean it was right. And yet you gave me this amazing wedding."

"Well, I used your credit card." Bridgett smiled.

And for the first time, Scarlett didn't feel like the afterthought.

Duncan had loved her, just as he said. And she did have a good life. She'd been raised by parents who loved her, despite the demands of their lives, and an aunt who let her into her world, however pained. For the past ten years she'd had a job she'd enjoyed, friends, a home. And that was the point, wasn't it? Just because she didn't have fame and fortune or a face that graced magazine covers, that didn't mean she had nothing. Didn't mean she *was* nothing.

She'd had everything she needed. She glanced at Luke. And now, because God had given her the wrong—or perhaps right—taxi, she had everything she wanted.

Huh.

Maybe she'd never been forgotten after all.

"I'll walk you down the aisle, sis."

Bridgett drew in a breath. "I'm so sorry, Scarlett. And so lucky to have you. Thank you."

"Now, clean up those tears, because you're getting married." Scarlett held out her arm.

She led her sister to the top of the aisle, and as Bridgett smiled at her groom, Scarlett bent down to straighten her dress. She looked at Luke. "You coming?"

"I'm not looking for a part-time gig, you know." Luke was standing away from her a bit, the sun behind him like a halo.

"So, does that mean this is more than a job to you? That you want to be my wedding date?"

Then the music began to play. She turned to take her

sister's arm, but Luke walked forward and caught her. Then he cupped her cheek and leaned in. Luke kissed her, leaving behind his scent—the sense of danger, of adventure, of a Caribbean romance.

"I do, Scarlett. Oh, I really do."

EPILOGUE

Someone should probably wake her up, because this kind of dreaming could get her into trouble. Too many hopes wrapped up in seeing herself standing at the top of the aisle, Luke resplendent in his tuxedo as he stood at the altar. And next to him, his well-attired pals from Stryker International, the ones who had swooped in for the rescue in Cancun. Scarlett recognized, even in her sleep, Chet, with his dark, short-cropped hair. His beautiful wife, Mae, with her red mane tied back, was sitting on the groom's side, her hands on her rounded belly. Beside Chet stood his pal Vicktor, his angular Russian features a contrast to his pretty blonde wife, Gracie, who rocked their little boy, now almost a year old. Brody, tall and stern, had his gaze on his extravagant—and famous—wife, Ronie, who had just released another blues album, now climbing the charts. The pop-turned-blues star was sitting beside Gracie, and cooing at little VJ—Vicktor Junior, as she called him.

On the bride's side sat Duncan, his arm across the pew, smiling at Bridgett, standing at the end of the aisle, grinning up at the bride.

At Scarlett.

She loved this moment in the dream when she might

convince herself it was real. When the sultry fragrance of the tropical breeze wove into the cabana, lifting her veil. When the music stirred the audience to turn, to look at her. When her bare feet tunneled into the soft, cool sand. When Luke looked up at her, nothing of the fear she'd remembered in his eyes.

Calm. Sure. Trusting. He had amazing eyes—she always remembered them, the kind that could find her fears, pull out a smile.

Make her trust him back.

No, she didn't want to wake up. Because waking up meant more phone calls, emails and the ache of knowing he lived on the other side of the world. The ache of having given him her heart so he could take it with him to Prague. Into his sometimes clandestine life.

Into the fear of not knowing where he might be. If he might be hurt. Or worse.

"I hate you doing this without me," she'd said on the phone. And in her dream. "I hate you leaving, and me not having a clue where you are."

"I know. This isn't forever. Like I said, this isn't a part-time gig for me."

But it felt like forever. Six months of online dating? And meanwhile, she'd returned to her temporary life. Only, well, it wasn't so temporary anymore, was it? Not with her quitting her temp jobs and hiring on full-time at the animal shelter. Okay, yes, she also worked one day a week at the bookstore, but that was only for the free books.

Which she had better start reading soon. Her to-be-read pile towered beside her bed, a casualty of her late-night chats with Luke.

From wherever he checked in from around the world.

Having adventures without her.

She saw herself again at the top of the aisle, the music swelling around her.

"Scarlett?"

She felt the heat of breath on her face, the scratch against her cheek. Put her hand up even as she saw him in her dream, a slow grin sliding up his face.

"Scarlett, it's time to wake up."

No. Please. "No."

She rolled over, trying to recapture the dream. To recapture herself walking down the aisle, into his arms. Into his life.

"Honey, really. We have to go."

Go… She drew in a quick breath. Opened her eyes.

Luke sat beside her, brushing her hair from her face. "Sorry to wake you, but the honeymoon is over. We have to catch a flight back to Prague in three hours."

Honeymoon.

She caught his hand on her face. "It wasn't a dream."

"Huh?" He appeared bronzed by the sun, his eyes shining, his burnished brown hair tousled by sleep. "What wasn't a dream?"

"The wedding. Our life together. We really did get married."

He ran his thumb over his lips. "Yes, we did. But as for the dream?" He stretched out beside her, touching his lips to hers. "I think it is just the beginning."

* * * * *

Dear Reader,

The first time I went to Isla Mujeres, I knew I had to write a book set there. If you're looking for a quaint and quiet place to vacation, this is a fun spot off the coast of Cancun. Just don't go when Luke and Scarlett are there! I was captured with the idea of the wrong bridesmaid at a destination wedding—and what would happen if she found herself in her own "action-adventure" novel. I also loved the idea of what Luke might do—caught between needing her help and wanting to keep her safe. I couldn't escape the idea that, indeed, she might save him, too. A great relationship is about trust. We can't live our lives in fear that we will be betrayed. Doesn't it feel good when someone we love comes through for us? Here's hoping you have people you trust in your life.

Susan May Warren

QUESTIONS FOR DISCUSSION

1. Scarlett is asked to fill in last minute at her sister's wedding. How many weddings have you been in, and what is your worst/best memory?

2. Have you ever been set up, either at a wedding or otherwise? Describe your experience.

3. The wedding is a destination wedding in Mexico. Have you ever been to a foreign wedding? Was it frightening or did you feel safe?

4. Have you ever been mistaken for someone else?

5. Scarlett regrets saying no to helping Lucia. Why? Have you ever wanted to do something out of the ordinary, even dangerous?

6. Luke doesn't want to involve Scarlett, but he has to because of Lucia's safety. Have you ever had to ask someone to do something difficult, something you didn't want them to do?

7. Lucia really loves Benito, but she planned to betray him. Have you ever had to betray someone you loved for a greater good? What would you have done in Lucia's place?

8. Scarlett is accused of something she didn't do, in order to get her away from the Sanchez family. Although it is for her good, it still hurts her. Have

you ever been accused of something you didn't do? Did you defend yourself?

9. Scarlett discovers that, indeed, Duncan did love her. Have you ever discovered, after the fact, that someone cared for you but didn't ever tell you? Have you ever loved someone but never told them? Do you regret it?

10. Luke has a dark secret that keeps him from trusting anyone. What is it? What happens that allows him to trust again? Do you have any mistakes in your past that you find difficult to move forward from? Have you succeeded?

11. What does Scarlett realize about her role in her wedding? Have you held back from celebrating with someone you love because of personal frustrations?

12. Bridgett and Scarlett struggled in their different roles in the family. Do you have a sibling, maybe one who has succeeded in an area where you might have struggled? Do you feel as though you live in the shadows of your siblings? Or are you the "famous" one? How does that feel?

INSPIRATIONAL

Inspirational romances to warm your heart & soul.

Love Inspired®
SUSPENSE

TITLES AVAILABLE NEXT MONTH

Available June 14, 2011

PROTECTING HER OWN
Guardians, Inc.
Margaret Daley

OUT OF TIME
Texas Ranger Justice
Shirlee McCoy

LAWMAN-IN-CHARGE
Laura Scott

BEHIND THE BADGE
Susan Sleeman

LISCNM0511

REQUEST YOUR FREE BOOKS!

2 FREE RIVETING INSPIRATIONAL NOVELS PLUS 2 FREE MYSTERY GIFTS

Love Inspired®
SUSPENSE

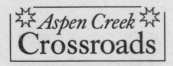